I0690574

THE BRAZILIAN

First Edition

Published by The Nazca Plains Corporation
Las Vegas, Nevada
2009

ISBN: 978-1-935509-60-8

Published by

The Nazca Plains Corporation ®
4640 Paradise Rd, Suite 141
Las Vegas NV 89109-8000

PUBLISHER'S NOTE
The Brazilian is a work of fiction created wholly by *Bill Smith*'s
imagination. All characters are fictional and any resemblance to any
persons living or deceased is purely by accident. No portion of this
book reflects any real person or events.

Cover Photos, Raisa Kanareva and Micha
Art Director, Blake Stephens

DEDICATION

To those who dream of having a slave collar around their neck and to those who dream of holding a slave whip in their hand.

THE BRAZILIAN

First Edition

Bill Smith

CHAPTER 1

I first met João at a luncheon in New York City. My brokerage firm, Schatts & Dunhill, was hosting an "appreciation" event for their 50 top clients. By pure chance, João de Silva and I, Christian Nelson, were seated next to each and I was instantly attracted to his dashing good looks, the charm that nobility seems to breed enhanced by his slightly accented English, and his intense interest in me as a person. It was seldom one finds a person who is obviously sincerely more interested in others than in themselves and João de Silva was one such person.

João looked to be about my own age - late 20s to early 30s, but he was so well built it was hard to tell really. The dress for the occasion was formal, but his tuxedo was obviously hand tailored in that it fit like a glove and nicely displayed his best assets, unusual in formal dress these days. He was about 6'2", around 190 pounds I would judge, very muscular from the way he carried himself, extremely handsome with creamy ivory colored very smooth skin, jet black hair worn long pulled back in a tight pony-tail, had large piercing jet-black eyes that matched his hair, had a waist that looked no more than 28" or so, a bubble-butted ass, and a bulging crotch that the cut of the trousers made no effort to hide, but indeed, seems to emphasize. He had the looks that commanded attention, people stared at without realizing it, and gave those so inclined, like me, a real hard-on. In other words, he was about as sexy as men get!

João wasn't one to be inhibited. Before we were seating, he took his time in looking me over rather openly and I saw him study my face, the body he imagined under the tuxedo, and especially my crotch where my undershorts had deliberately been cut to best display my rather ample package to advantage, striped tux pants or not.

Once we were seated, I was startled to feel his hand groping my crotch and, although I gasped a bit in surprise, I moved my legs apart to grant him easier access nevertheless.

"Nice," he whispered as he squeezed my package before returning his hand to the table. "Your visual sweep of my body before we were seated told me you approved of what you saw and that we could become good friends," he added so no one else could hear it. "Am I wrong, my American friend?"

I answered him by placing my hand under the table and rather languidly massaged his genitals which I found to be as hard as my own and even bigger than I thought they might be from my visual inspection.

This had to stop abruptly however, in that the appetizers were being served and the luncheon was underway. But we got to know each other in conversation. I quickly found out João de Silva was a Brazilian on a brief visit to New York City to attend to financial affairs. He found out I was about his age and a native of New York City. We both had considerable wealth or neither of us would be at this particular luncheon.

"What business are you in, Mr. de Silva," I probed.

"Call me João, please. Livestock, primarily," João answered. "And you, Mr. Nelson?"

"Christian, if you're João," I replied. "I'm not really into anything yet, João. My parents died in an accident about five years ago and left me with some assets, so I've been in no rush."

"Nevertheless, a person, especially young men our age, need something interesting to do," João said. "I love my business enterprise and find it absorbs almost all my time - time I enjoy and well-spent, I might add," João said with an engaging smile. He paused and then added with a twinkle in his eye, "and it fits right in with my personal preferences" without further explanation.

"I'm sort of disgusted with myself, Joáo, if I can be totally truthful. A man should be doing something worthwhile, something that helps society, and which he finds personally satisfying. I've tried volunteer work at one of the local hospitals, organized some fund-raising events for the local parish, and even set up a small business selling leather goods to the S&M boys here in the city. But none of it has held my interest very long," I explained.

"You're Catholic?" Joáo said, obviously pleased.

"Well, yes, but there's not a drop of a priest in me," I snickered. "The church and I have issues over who I take to my bed," I added as if I were making confession.

"I too am a token Catholic. Most Brazilians are, but the connection is very loose. The Church in Brazil is extremely tolerant of all sorts of things, especially if you drop them a nice donation now and then. What happened to your leather business?" Joáo asked.

"Oh, it was OK, but the profits were marginal, the customers were more into fantasy costuming than anything else, and it just seemed pointless after a while, especially if you didn't need the money to start with. I sold it at a loss to some old queen in Brooklyn who actually thinks he's performing a vital service to the good citizens of New York."

"Sounds like you're ripe to find yourself," Joáo said as his hand squeezed my thigh closest to him.

"I'm ready to go to bed with you," I replied, "if that's what you mean. We could go to my townhouse as soon as this damn thing is over," I suggested.

"That's an excellent idea," Joáo said, "and we can do that as you suggest. But that's not really what I meant. I was implying something much more engaging than a one-night stand between two handsome studs."

"What do you do that you find so interesting?" I replied. "Not that I'm letting you off the hook for a visit to my townhouse within the next half hour or so?"

"We'll go to your townhouse, all right, Christian, but when I said I was in the livestock business, I'm sure you thought cattle. Right?"

"Yes, isn't that what Brazil is noted for, among other things - those huge ranches with hundreds of thousands of cattle," I replied.

"We have those by the thousands, Christian, but there are other types of livestock that are in great demand now," João said quietly. "Brazil's been into it for the past 50 years in one form or another; America, by comparison, is relatively new to the market."

I pondered João's remarks for a moment and then it hit me.

"Mother of God, João, you're in the slave business," I exclaimed.

"Not just in it, Christian. I'm the leading producer in Brazil now. And, my friend, it's not only extremely profitable - especially now that the American market has opened up - but it's totally absorbing. Not to mention having your choice among literally thousands at any given time to amuse yourself with. Slaves are there to please their masters, Christian, and until you've bedded down a well-trained slaveboy, you really haven't explored the full gamut of sexual pleasure," João smiled knowingly. "I don't want to discredit the fun we'll have at your townhouse shortly, Christian, but, frankly, it just won't stack up with an eager slave at your disposal. Have you bedded a slave down yet, Christian? I know they're aren't too many in New York yet, but hundreds are being imported daily, not counting the home grown slaves the government is turning over from the overcrowded prisons and detention centers they've got everywhere."

I was so floored I found it difficult to answer João, but I did manage to mutter that I hadn't used a slave yet.

"Hell, João, I've only seen a handful of slaves in my whole lifetime and that's been in the past month when I drove by some road construction crew. I couldn't believe it when I saw a few naked men chained by their collars working alongside an overseer cracking a whip over their backside. I almost drove off the road staring at them. But I should have known I'd run into seeing them sooner or later. The papers are full of stories about prisoners being sold at auction, contractors snapping them up, and that sort of thing. There was even a story in the New York Times about a male brothel opening up in Manhattan stocked with some imported slaves in their early twenties. I couldn't even fathom it."

"You are naive, Christian," Joáo chuckled. "The availability of slaves will open up all sorts of new possibilities for American enterprise, I'm sure. The demand will grow astronomically as soon as you Yankees realize the uses human livestock can be put to. The secret is to be on the supply end of the business. A friend of mine in Paraguay has somehow or other got a monopoly on the supply of slaves there and made almost a billion dollars pure profit in the first five years. And Paraguay's peanuts compared to Brazil or the United States."

I had lost all interest in the delicious food before us - even the handsome waiters serving the food in the tightest pants decorum would allow for a respectable catering company. Even the thought of having the handsome well-hung Brazilian in my bed within the hour faded in comparison to the whole new world he was presenting to me so enthusiastically.

We left the banquet as soon as was socially correct, each thanking our host profusely. Within 20 minutes we were in my townhouse bedroom stripped, our formal clothes scattered on the floor along with our underclothes, socks, shoes, and everything else. Joáo's body was even better than I thought it would be when I sized him up at the banquet and he obviously approved of my body once it was totally exposed. Both of us sported huge erections even before we had ripped our shirts off and pre-cum was dripping from Joáo's prick as he took my body in now that it was fully displayed. Joáo's prick was even larger than I surmised - it was long and exceptionally thick, a good five inches in circumference I judged now that it was fully erect.

An hour later, we were exhausted and both of us totally drained. We had sucked each other until full loads were swallowed into our stomachs, fucked each other twice after greasing each other's holes, and sucked on our partner's nipples until each of us were swollen and sore. We reeked of animal sweat, each of us had a few scratches on our backs from moments of raw passion, and our lips were swollen from some intense kissing and tongue probing. Neither of us exhibited the slightest twinge of inhibition or hesitancy in doing everything possible even though we had known each other for less than three hours maximum. There wasn't one iota of each other's bodies that was foreign to us now, including our assholes, our mouths, our rampant pricks, and our swollen balls.

Being fucked by João was a unique experience, even for me who was a long way from being a virgin, having experienced hundreds of one-night stands, bar pickups, and hired hustlers over the past few years. João was exceptionally masterful in ramming his organ completely down your throat, holding your head in a vise-like grip as he did so - and even more demanding when he pistoned his large organ completely up my asschute upon entry and then fucked me with such dominance I was actually scooted up against the bed's headboard. If my hole hadn't been well stretched by numerous men over the years, João would have been more than I could have handled and his assault on my body would be more like a painful rape than an enjoyable fuck. He literally treated my body as if he owned it and was going to extract the last ounce of pleasure that body could produce for him. The experience was exhilarating, but weird nonetheless. I'd certainly never experienced anything like it.

"No slave could be better than you, João, no matter how much training he might have had," I ventured in appreciation of João's well-honed skills in a man's bed.

"I might say the same for you, Christian," João said with sincere appreciation, "but I really can't, my friend. Neither of us can compete with a slave's motivation."

"Motivation?" I asked.

"A slave knows he has to please his master like no other. Anything less and he'll be put in a situation he'll deeply regret. That raw fear is a powerful motivator - about as strong as a motivator can be. After a while, though, the slave forgets about his fear and gives his master upmost pleasure out of pure habit and to insure his master will keep him."

"And what is a situation he'll deeply regret, as you put it, João?" I asked rather innocently.

"Unfathomable physical pain would be the mildest, but being sold off to a far worse situation is the primary motivator. It's far better to offer a master the best fuck he's ever had than to be sold to a Brazilian mine where you'll never see light again and your life span under the constant whips is less than a year or so. Slaves aren't stupid - they evaluate their options and then decide the best course to take. Those boys sold to the new brothel opening in Manhattan - that's nothing compared to the underground gold mines in Peru or turning sewage into fertilizer outside Rio where the smell alone is enough to kill you, let alone standing in shit 14 to 15 hours a day under a sadistic whipmaster who gets his jollies beating you to death."

I soaked up his vivid scenario. "I see your point, Joáo," I said. "I suppose I'm terribly naive when it comes to slavery. It's just I have no experience with it to date."

"You will, my friend. You can't help it. America will respond to the new opportunities just like all the other countries who are ahead of them in this area. It won't be a decade until there will be five times more slaves in this country than free men, mark my words. That's the way it is in Brazil, Saudi Arabia, Malaysia, Mexico, and most other countries that have seized the opportunity to march ahead," Joáo explained.

"That's what our biggest corporations are claiming, Joáo," I offered, "so you're not alone in your predictions."

"Well, Christian, we get along well," Joáo said as he grabbed my prick once again and started stroking me. "And you seem to like me as far as I can tell. Tell you what, Christian. I'll invite you to go home with me and I'll show you first hand just how this slavery thing plays out in real life. You buy the plane tickets for the two of us - I'll furnish the bed and board and throw in some slaveboys for your amusement, as many as you can handle, to boot. How about it? You can't beat an offer like that - a rich boy from South America helping out an obviously rich boy from New York, both of whom have nice bodies, are gay, and open to adventure and purposeful pursuits. Especially for a poor lost soul looking for a purpose to his life," Joáo laughed before his mouth closed around my dick once again.

Two days later, Joáo and I landed at the nearest airport to his livestock ranch. We took a non-stop to Sao Paulo first-class and then transferred to a turboprop to the city of Campinos in southeast Brazil. His Porshe SUV picked us up there and began the 120 mile trip on dirt roads to his huge ranch, located well in the Brazilian out-country, part jungle and part steppes.

The road trip was relatively slow, but his slave chauffeur had fixed us a beautiful meal arranged in a hamper located between us in the back seat, complete with chilled wine and a delicious custard-like dessert served out of an ice-pack to assure the right temperature.

But it was the chauffeur himself that was the real treat: a 6" jet-black boy obviously around 20 or so with a beautiful face, the smoothest skin I've even seen, close-cropped black hair, a well-muscled, well-defined torso and beautifully shaped and very large always at least semi-erect sexual organs on full display at all times since his only clothing was a thick brass collar around his neck, large tit rings installed in both tits, and a thick one-inch band around his ball sac and the base of his prick to assure a prominent display of his genitals at all times. It was the first slave I'd ever seen up close like this and this boy would have turned anyone on - especially being displayed like he was. I couldn't imagine how the slave must feel being made to parade around naked like this in public, especially fitted out with the metal accouterments that emphasized his slave status. And, more overwhelmingly, I couldn't imagine actually owning a body like this - a body I could do anything I wanted with since it was nothing more than an owner's property.

Joáo saw me ogling the slave chauffeur from the moment I first spotted him holding the back door of the SUV open for us.

"Don't worry, Christian. If you can hold off until we get to the ranch, he's all yours for as long as you want. But you may see something else you like better once we get to the estate. If so, don't hesitate. Every slave on the place understands he's there to serve not only me but any guest to the ranch as well. In fact, it's viewed as a real honor to get chosen to service one of the master's guests."

I enjoyed the delicious meal en route, but maintained a full erection the whole time thinking of the young man driving us down the road quietly, but I didn't miss his furtive inviting glances in the rear-view mirror whenever his master was looking out the side window. God, was this the good life or what?

CHAPTER 2

The jet-black chauffeur was as good as he looked once I had him in my bed at Joáo's ranch. He was compliant, yet inventive; submissive, yet fully participatory; eager to please, yet seemingly inexhaustible. I had fucked his beautiful backside four times by the time it was morning, each time where he had sucked me to the point of orgasm prior to my ordering him onto his back with his legs raised over my shoulders. I delighted in looking into his accepting eyes as I rammed into him as far as possible and then humped him hard until I couldn't hold back any longer and filled his rectum with load after load of my cum.

"Would you like me to gently suck you?" constituted the first words of the day from the smiling slave, his mouth hovering over my erect prick as I slowly awoke. "Or empty your bladder?" he added enthusiastically, as if drinking piss was a great treat.

As my eyes focused, I saw the black beauty as eager as ever despite the sweat dried on his body after last night's exertions, a strong smell of rutting in the room, and a steady stream of thick white cum leaking out of his asshole, clearly visible on his jet-black thighs.

"No, you need to wash yourself," I commented, nodding toward the adjacent bathroom.

"Yes, master," he replied as he quickly headed for the bathroom and, within moments, I heard the unmistakable sound of a person flushing their innards followed quickly by the sound of a bidet flushing and then a shower going in full operation.

Within minutes, he returned with his body still glistening from the water and quickly assumed an inviting position on all fours with his legs far apart so his hole was fully exposed.

"Would master like to fuck me now? I've cleaned my body as you commanded, master, and prepared myself for your use," referring to the fresh K-Y visible around his hole.

Who could resist an invitation like that, especially by a body so beautiful it would be impossible to improve. I entered him slowly but deeply, and started to pump him slowly as I settled onto his back and placed my hands on his muscular pecs so I could play with his tits as I fucked him.

"Thank you, master," was the black's response to the invasion of his body and he began to gently push back to my thrusts so I could penetrate him as far as possible. This was coupled with a rhythmic tightening of his ass muscles to heighten his user's pleasure yielding a sensation I was being pumped to new heights of sexual satisfaction.

Within minutes I discharged a huge load far up his chute, squeezing and twisting his nipples as the orgasm rippled through me. The slave writhing beneath me groaned quietly from the pain caused by the nipple play but never moved from my grip; I moaned in raw ecstasy as my balls drained into the body beneath me.

"Christian, are you going to fuck Niger all day or would you like a little breakfast followed by a starter tour of the ranch?" Joáo shouted from the other side of the bedroom door. "Doesn't matter one way or the other, I just need to make plans for the day."

"Give me a moment to shower and I'll join you for breakfast, Joáo," I yelled back, still molded onto the slave's back.

"Fine, see you in 15 minutes down in the main dining room - just throw anything on - a pair of shorts and a T-shirt will do fine. Looks like it might be hot and steamy today so dress accordingly."

I heard footsteps going down the hall outside while I stopped playing with the black slave's nipple rings and "unglued" myself from the boy's smooth back as I slowly slipped out of his hole.

"So you're named Niger," I said, patting the slave on his butt in dismissal.

"Yes, master. My master named me that when he first obtained me a few years ago. It means 'black' in Portuguese."

"How come you speak English?" I asked.

"I'm from Mississippi originally, master. It's Portuguese I had to learn."

"Mississippi?" I asked in astonishment. "What are you doing down here?"

"It's not that unusual, Master. But you need to get ready for breakfast. I'll tell you my humble little story when you have time, Master, if that's alright with you. Ask for me tonight and I'll tell you everything you want to know, if it would please you, Master."

"You're something in bed, Niger," I mumbled as I headed for the bathroom.

"Thank you, Master," the black slave responded, obviously relieved. "I'm happy I was able to please you, Master," the slave went on, "but I can be even better tonight if you ask for Niger," he added, almost pleading.

When I got out of the shower, the black slave had disappeared, but the bed had clean linens and the room was spotless. My clothes had been unpacked and were hanging in the closet with the exception of fresh underwear, shorts and a pullover along with my socks and shoes which were neatly arranged on the bed. Apparently, Niger listened carefully to every suggestion his master made.

When I arrived in the dining room, Joáo was awaiting me reading the morning newspaper and sipping some fragrant coffee. Behind him against the wall, standing erect with their hands behind their back and their heads bowed, were two attendants: the first was a totally naked male in his early 20s, completely body shaved below his neck and fitted with tit rings, a genital band forcing his organs into a showy protrusion, and a tall slave collar that forced his head into an upright position. Although tanned all over, he was obviously a white boy, complete with blond hair allowed to grow down to his neck and bright green eyes. He wasn't particularly tall, about 5"7", but was muscular and compact without an ounce of fat on him. The other attendant was fully clothed: a female also appearing to be in her early 20s, obviously well into a pregnancy, and also a pure white, judging from her red hair and hazel eyes. Her clothing consisted of a gown that reached the floor and covered her completely, although her neck collar and ankle bracelets were clearly visible, along with her bare feet.

Both slaves, in their own ways, were stand-outs: one a paradigm of masculinity- well muscled, rugged, and heavily hung; the other the epitome of the best of her gender - buxom, curvaceous, and pretty.

As João saw me studying the pair, he chuckled.

"We use the breeding stock in full work assignments, so most of the females you'll see will be pregnant or have just been," he said. "A brood like this one can have a yield of 15 to 20 new products if we schedule it properly. And the stud can do his duties at night once he's finished his regular work assignments. If we utilize him efficiently, he can produce a good 1500 to 2000 pregnancies before he dries up," João explained.

I stopped in my tracks and took in the impact of João's words.

"You breed slaves?" I asked in utter astonishment.

"Of course, Christian. Everyone does nowadays. Where do you think the majority of slaves come from, anyway?" João chuckled.

"Well, I thought they were prisoners sold by the government or prisoners of war," I answered. "That's all I've ever heard of."

"That's where the supply usually starts when a country first reintroduces slavery, but that source doesn't begin to meet the demand once the idea of slavery catches on. In the United States, it won't be long until the prisons, jails, drug clinics, juvenile detention centers, and reformatories are completely emptied and the prisoners of war are sold practically before they get them unloaded, so when the market demands more you can only do three things basically: (1) expand the criminal law so more of the populace is imprisoned and hence up for sale; (2) import them in masses; or (3) breed them. The first two I mentioned have their limitations; the last doesn't - you can breed as many as you need once the operation is firmly in place and it's the cheapest solution of the three options when you include the training considerations and the fact you can selectively breed toward an attractive sales product."

I felt like I was on another planet somehow as João spoke so casually about breeding people for a marketplace as if they were cattle. I remained standing, dumbfounded, but noticed both slave attendants had blushed a deep shade of red as their role in all this was discussed so openly in front of them.

"Take Thor here, for example," João said as he snapped his finger and the blond slave leaped to his side whereupon his master grabbed his ringed penis and began stroking him languidly as the huge organ grew in his hand. "This boy has already sired well over 400 stock for our pens and he's just getting started - a good number of them blond, 60% male to date, and all well built and sturdy. When they're sold off, they will know nothing but slavery and be totally compliance to their new life. Thor here came to us from an Argentine prison - wild and unruly even though he was just a little over 18 when we bought him. A few months of serious training, the realization that he would either come around or die in the process including experiencing some real pain for the first time in his life, taught him he wasn't in control of his life anymore and his body belonged to whoever bought him. By the time he was 19, we put him to stud and the rest is history," João smiled as the slave broke out in a sweat trying desperately to control shooting off in his master's hand. "Steady there, Thor. You know you have to save your spunk for the rutting bench tonight."

"Yes, master," Thor answered in Portuguese as he struggled to control his body, pressing his lips together as he tried to keep the pending eruption within him. His humiliation and shame at being fondled like this in front of a total stranger, let alone his role in studding new 'products' into being like a prize horse, went unstated outside a small tear working its way down his cheek.

"Despite everything, Thor's still got some emotion left in him - makes him interesting. But it doesn't do him one bit of good, does it, Thor? Frankly, I enjoy watching a slave do things he doesn't necessarily want to do but knows he has no choice. After all, that's the essence of being a slave, isn't it? Performing to your owner's desires, not your own! Isn't that so, Thor?"

"Yes, Master," the blond slave promptly replied as Thor let loose of his banded organ and dismissed him with a slap to his butt.

The slave promptly returned to his position by the wall with his hands behind his back, his prick still rampant.

"Would you like to fuck Thor after supper, Christian? We can always readjust his studding schedule if you'd like him," João offered.

"I think I'll take a raincheck on that one, João," I replied rather confused at all this man-flesh available apparently on a whim. "Your black chauffeur pretty well drained me last night," I confessed, finding it strange I would discuss such intimate details with a man I had just met two days ago.

"Well, whatever you want, Christian, although I must say this slave's ass offers up a damn good fuck. Had him myself just a few days ago." The slave under discussion blushed deep red in humiliation as his master's use of his body was advertised.

"In that case, Thor, now that I've got you all ready, you trot yourself down to the rutting pens and the studmaster can put you to that black wench I selected for you yesterday. No use not getting started on the wench and then the studmaster can use you again later this evening. We can have our coffee without the likes of you stinking up the place here. Felicity can wait on us all by herself, can't you, girl?"

"Yes, master," the red-haired slave wench replied humbly.

As Thor quickly started to leave, João added: "Thor, you hump that black wench good, you hear. I'm planning on a nice brown-colored pup out of that one - two if you hump her good and hard. Remember, you get a day off if you produce twins," he laughed as the blond slave nodded and left with the usual "Yes, Master."

"Christian, don't just stand there. Sit down and enjoy a cup of coffee. We raise it right here on the estate and it's especially good if I do say so myself. I know all of this is new to you and it will take you a while to get to know how all of this works, but relax and just let it all soak in. Besides, Christian, you must be a little worn out from the long trip. I know I am, despite having a nice sandy-haired boy in my bed just fresh out of training."

"Well, it will probably take a day or two to get back to normal," I admitted.

"How about we just talk a bit about what we actually do here at the ranch and how slavery works here in Brazil. That way neither one of us has to do much other than talk and listen and Felicity here can fix us a meal when we're hungry. We can always tour the place when we're up to it, although I must warn you, Christian, this place is huge and we perform many functions here - everything from breeding them, as you just heard - to 'breaking in' new stock that was formerly free - to processing new prison stock - well, it just goes on and on. But each aspect is mighty profitable or we'd close it down. You want to make real money - listen and learn, Christian!"

"Sounds great if you have the time, Joáo," I replied. "I'm surprised how interested I am in all this. Maybe you're right - I need a purpose to my life."

"Everyone does, Christian, even a slave. That's what we give them here at the ranch - a purpose in life - and we can do the same for you, but from the other side of things - the owner's side, that is," Joáo said forcefully as he had another sip of his coffee and selected a small freshly-baked cinnamon roll to munch on, coated with an unusual white sauce on top.

"Know what we top these rolls off with?" Joáo asked as he took a good bite into the breakfast offering.

"Jesus, Joáo, how would I know about baking a roll?" Christian asked rather defensively. "I can't cook."

"No, Christian, I'm talking about this creamy sauce on top," Joáo chuckled.

"Haven't a clue, Joáo," Christian said as he took his first sip of coffee.

"Fresh cum, Christian. It's delicious when it's real fresh and from studs still in the prime of their youth. We keep a fresh slaveboy in the kitchen at all times just so the cook can get all the cum they want at any time. It's great for toppings, sauces, condiments, or just a refreshing drink in itself."

"Never tried in on food, Joáo," I replied. "In fact, I never heard of using cum for anything like that."

"That's why you're here, Christian. To explore and learn," Joáo said with some satisfaction as he carefully took another bite of his roll dripping with the special icing. "Yum! Damn, that's good. I really think black slave boys just under 20 have the best sauce available. That's where this came from. This particular milk stud is one of my favorites. Try it, Christian, you won't believe how good it is mixed with the cinnamon taste."

I wasn't adverse to swallowing cum as João already knew, having had several full loads out of him slide down my throat just two nights ago. I picked up one of the rolls and sopped it in some excess sauce that had run down the side before taking a big bite.

"That is good, João," I said as I savored it in my mouth. "Creamy but with a nice tang to it. That boy in your kitchen ever get tired of being milked?"

"I don't know that anyone ever asked him," João laughed. "But we only empty his balls three or four times a day usually - unless we're having a big party or something. Any we don't use within an hour or so, we store in the refrigerator and use in cooked dishes of one type or another."

"How long does a milk stud like that last?" I asked out of curiosity.

"I don't know, Christian. When they turn 21, we assign them other duties in that my cook demands only cum from boys 18 to 21 years old. The cook claims it tends to get bitter after that."

"I'll remember that when I start up a restaurant back in New York," I chuckled. "It will be the secret ingredient that will beat out all the competition. And here I thought cum was only good when you extracted it yourself with a great blow job."

"Broaden your horizons, Christian. That's why I invited you down here."

We both helped ourselves to another roll dripping with the special sauce and then another, washing it down with the delicious coffee before settling back for some serious discussion.

João started out discussing selling the finished product, mainly to those wealthy enough to afford anything they wanted. Selling the most select slaves available was his specialty. It seemed every new buyer wanted at least one strikingly handsome slave to keep his house neat and clean at all times, serve as his personal valet, but for other purposes as well, namely serving as a walking status symbol, a property others envied, and usually to bring them and their friends unparalleled pleasures in the sexual arena.

Consequently, João's sales outlet offered only the very best bodies the market could produce, the highest trained slaves ever accomplished, and properties that others not only coveted but were so rare others could never hope to afford them.

"Like Niger and Thor?" I asked, since they were only two of Joáo's properties I had seen up close and naked.

"Yes, Christian. For example, I match my slaves to my cars. The Porshe's exterior paint is the same shade as the slave's hide, e.g., jet-black and the Porshe is trimmed in nickel chromium that exactly matches Niger's body fittings (collar, tit, nose, and ear rings, and genital band). I ordered that Porshe SUV directly from the factory in African black upholstered with black horsehide that exactly matches Niger's hide. For my other cars, I have a Jaguar upholstered in Siberian Tiger hides (an endangered species), driven by an ivory colored slave whose hide exactly matches the exterior paint; a gleaming snow-white Bentley fitted out with dark brown leather and a dark brown African slave chauffeur whose hide exactly matches the leather interior; a opalescent light brown Range Rover with a chauffeur who has the smoothest creamiest light brown skin a person has ever seen which exactly matches the exterior paint; and a fire-engine red Jeep with a calico cat interior and a mulatto slave with blotchy patches of black and white all over him that compliments the calico interior.

"All of these customized options cost a great deal extra, but when you're already paying over $100,000 for a car, what's a little more if you get exactly what you want, especially when the slave going with it costs as much or more than the car generally.

"One of my customers really admired my stable of cars with their matching drivers, and he wanted a new Maybach to be upholstered in slave hide the exact shade as the slave who would be driving it - jet black with gold trim. When I faxed this unusual request into the Maybach factory in Germany, I got a long reply. They stated they had done this before for several Middle Eastern customers and knew exactly what the parameters were. The current model took 38 slave hides to cover the seats as well as the dash, roof lining, door panels, and arm rests. Exactly matched, this required a search of world markets taking several weeks and the costs generally added $3.04 million to the price of the car since 38 slaves matched for color with suitable hides for tanning were running about $80,000 each if they limited those purchased to those well over 33 years of age, the type of slave typically selected for this purpose. Slaves in their prime (18 to 22 years old) would add an astounding $9,500,000 to the costs of the car, an absurd expense in their eyes. Purchasers who had all the seats upholstered in slave hide had expressed disappointment over time - slave hide did not hold up well to the constant flexing and stressing common in automobile seats - and the seats too easily got puncture holes or cracked over time. Therefore, they recommended cowhide dyed to exactly match the slave hide which would be utilized only in more suitable surfaces not subject to flexing stress. Maybachs with slave hide door panels, head rests, arm rests, dash, sun visors, and roof lining took only 18 hides and meshed well with the cowhide utilized in all seating surfaces. Maybachs so fitted out cost $1.44 million extra if older slaves were utilized in the selection of hides. They argued that older slave hides worked out better in fitting out the car since the skin was already well stretched, tended to be considerably thicker than those in the 18-22 year range, and often had interesting brand burns and whip scars that clearly identified the hide for what it was and added considerable interest. They said, unless instructed otherwise, they would upholster where brand and whip marks were well featured, although, of course, a customer could request these hide marks not show if they preferred.

"When I shared these observations from the Maybach factory with my customer, he immediately agreed with their recommendations as long as the car was outfitted to match the slave chauffeur he was purchasing from me. The slave I sold him was a hugely muscular and strikingly handsome black with a hairless body below the eyebrows, brilliant blue eyes, thin lips, a prominent jaw line, high cheekbones, and a straight Grecian nose. He had magnificent pecs, abs, and a muscular bubble butt along with beautifully shaped and very large genitals, including a neatly circumcised 10" penis. I agreed to fit him out with a tight fitting, 3" gold-plated collar, matching 2" tit rings, a matching tight fitting 2" genital band, and a matching 1" nose ring fitted through his septum that would rest right above his thin upper lip. The Maybach was ordered in jet black (to exactly match the slave's hide) with a gold-plated grille and bumpers, door handles, and antennae. The pair would create a sensation anywhere they appeared.

"As the customer signed the purchase agreement and gave me a check covering the costs of both the car (which I had ordered for him) and the slave ($325,000 for the car plus $1.440,000 for the slave hides plus $428,000 for the slave chauffeur fully fitted for a total of $2,293,000) I reminded him he was actually buying 19 slaves - one that would drive and take care of the car and 18 others, not quite so pretty probably, who he would be looking at (at least part of them) every time he got in the car.

"Almost 2.3 million for a damn car and one slave, João?" I asked incredulously

"Yes, Christian, but the chauffeur slave that wasn't upholstery is prime stock - he was just 19 and he could be fucked and do all the sucking his new owner and his friends wanted any time he wasn't driving the car."

"And be a sensation wherever they were parked," I added, "especially if, like Niger, he was ordered to show hard while he's displaying his body."

"Yes, Christian. The black slave was most showy anyway, but that prick of his - it really set him off," João reflected.

"But I digress, Christian," João said. "Let me get back to the art of selling stock.

"Some buyers are turned off by slaves they consider 'too handsome,' complaining they don't look masculine. For those, we offer a few slaves that are almost brutish in their appearance and by no standards would be considered handsome, let alone beautiful. But these slaves, usually priced considerably lower, are certainly masculine and we make sure they are well trained to satisfy every possible demand that might be made of them. Some masters just want a slave with excellent oral skills and could care less what the face sucking them looks like - they're interested in the throat action and the actual sucking skills the slave has. Others, particularly mistresses, like a slave heavy hung and very well built but who have faces that could never be mistaken as being feminine or 'smooth.' Again, we just make sure the slaves under consideration understand exactly why they are being purchased and what their new owners want them to do without the necessity of having to be told what to do each and every time. A slave who can anticipate what an owner wants and does it to perfection is seldom returned and is often valued for just what he is: a sex machine that doesn't disappoint!

"Every slave sold in the markets today, even the cheapest pieces of meat sold in public stalls, is thoroughly trained in how to please an owner sexually since sexual use of their bodies is often the main reason for buying them. Even the relatively poor can now, with a good credit rating or the self-discipline to save, can buy a slave in the $50,000 range. What he or she gets for that price is usually a slave not very good looking - certainly not strikingly handsome, a slave not in his prime years (18-24), and a slave with some bodily imperfections. But that doesn't preclude obtaining a slave well trained, well equipped, and willing to do anything necessary to please an owner in exchange for being bought, fed, and housed. For many slaves in this price range, ownership brings with it security, pride of being owned, and freedom from starving to death.

"Compared to their lives before being purchased, it's a fair exchange and slaves like this settle in early to the expectations their new owners have for them, whether it's taking a big one up their backside three or four times a day from their new master and/or his friends and business acquaintances, spending considerable time on their knees orally servicing their new owner, or bringing their new mistress the pleasures only possible when you own your sex partner outright and can command exactly what you want and get it time after time.

"Of course, they usually do a lot of other things as well: housekeeping, laundry; car-washing; gardening; repair work; construction, etc. Some work in factories on lease from their owners during the normal work hours; others are frequently hired out to contractors as manual laborers during the day; while still others are leased out as janitors, mechanics, farm workers, etc. But such assignments keep their bodies in great shape and simply make them all the more appealing once they return to their master's or mistress' home in that they are ready to be of service (most day jobs didn't allow any sexual outlets), they get fed at their home base, and that's where they eventually get a cage or pen to call home. No matter where a slave is assigned to work, their loyalty is always with the person who has bought them, beds them, and gives them a cage to sleep in. Being used for sexual pleasure is a small price to pay for all of that!"

"João, you make it all sound so logical," I said as I helped myself to another cum-soaked cinnamon roll and washed it down with the rich blend of coffee. "I feel like I'm in an alternate universe. New York seems so far away."

"Christian, you're like so many of my American customers. You're so removed from the 'real' world your ideas about slaves and the system that produces them are incredibly naive. I'm constantly deluged with questions from my American customers about the origins of the stock I sell, where they are obtained, whether the slaves know what their owners expect out of them, how the slaves accept their new status as property, how they are trained, whether there is a danger the slaves will rebel or run away, and how many people have owned the stock before."

"Well, I am naive, as you put it, João. But so are most Americans. Remember, slavery is a new thing to us. But that doesn't mean we're not curious about these things," I replied rather defensibly. "It doesn't mean we're dumb or anything."

"I'm sure you're not," João laughed.

"Human livestock doesn't just float down from heaven, you know," he chuckled, "or we'll all be doing our own dirty work and getting used to taking care of our own sex needs. But I can see your problem. A lot of people able to afford slaves probably think they're in the markets to be bought as if my magic. Actually, Christian, I get some of the same questions from most other nationalities too, especially where slavery is less than a generation or so old and isn't pervasive in their home country yet. So much so that I've prepared a short DVD on the whole subject that I'll be glad to show you today while we're resting and even make a copy for you to take home with you if you want to look at it again later. The presentation just tells a little about a few of the sources of slaves, a little about their preparation and training, a little about who buys them and where, and winds up with a little about their uses once they are sold. Would you like to see it?"

"Sounds good, João, and I'm sure I'll like a copy of the DVD if you're willing to share."

"No problem, Christian. The large screen TV is in the sales room just a few doors from here so we can see it right now. We can have a beer or whatever you like while we're watching the little show."

With that, we proceeded to the luxurious sales room next door to Joáo's main manor house and sunk down into some very comfortable arm chairs as a couple of really impressive naked slaves Joáo kept around as "house slaves" served us ice cold beers and then knelt down on all fours beside each of us so we could use their glistening, well-oiled backs as tables for our drinks.

CHAPTER 3

"You want one of the slaves to suck you off, Christian, while you're watching the presentation?" Joáo asked, "or is it too soon after Niger last night?

I looked at the two handsome slaves with their magnificent musculature and decided the offer was too good to resist.

"How about the black haired slave with the green eyes - he's a real looker," I replied.

"Fine," Joáo replied with a snap of his finger, whereupon the slave I mentioned crawled directly in front of me, his mouth opened in readiness, and the other slave, a beautiful black boy, crawled between us so we could both use his back as a table.

As Joáo pressed the start button, I felt fingers opening the zipper of my shorts, extracting my semi-erect organ, and a velvety mouth close around the end of my prick before quickly swallowing the entire shaft.

"The first part is on where slaves come from," Joáo explained as he reached down and began kneading the balls and huge prick of the black slave serving as our table.

I settled back in my chair to enjoy both the projected images and the expert mouth service from the gorgeous slave between my legs. Some dynamic music accompanied the presentation as I scooted down in my chair and spread my legs a little to give the slave better access. The presentation began as the green-eyed slave really got into his assigned task and I could feel the entire length of my prick being rhythmically massaged by the slave's well trained throat muscles.

The narration began as pictures began filling the screen in front of us.

"As you know, ladies and gentlemen, a significant and rapidly growing number of offerings in the current markets are bred specifically for their eventual sale so we'll start with how we breed slaves for the marketplace. That process all starts with the best genes available: slave studs carefully picked to produce the best prodigies mated with the best of slave broods who typically produce 15 to 20 pups during their peek reproduction period. The broods are only bred when they are optimally receptive - that five to seven day period every month when they're not pregnant. During that optimal period, a select stud mounts them repeatedly until they test out positive."

A huge banner appeared on the screen: "STUD SLAVES UTILIZED IN SLAVE BREEDING"

"Let's start by showing you some of examples of experienced stud slaves available in the marketplace currently - all with proven fertility and very high 'hit rates.' Most of them have sired at least 100 new slave pups prior to being offered on the open marketplace.

"The one shown now we purchased from a Brazilian dealer in Rio [the screen showed a photograph of a tall, well muscled, light brown man totally nude and fully body shaved with the exclusion of his eyebrows. His long, thick prick was fully erect between his legs as he hunched down with his knees spread wide to display his assets. Heavily collared and fitted with large tit rings, he stared directly into the screen with an eager look.] Well equipped for this job, he had already had 100 successful impregnations with breeding wenches before we purchased him. His previous owner had put him to the rutting benches starting at 18, so he's only 23 now and can produce hundreds more slave pups before he starts to falter.

He's eager to perform and prides himself on impregnating most anything placed under him."

"This next stud is a mulatto we bought off a St. Louis merchant [the screen showed a large dark brown man who was almost brutal looking with a thick muscular build and a very thick semi-erect prick.] This slave is himself the product of a large breeding farm in southern Missouri. His body and face are nothing exceptional, but his breeding organ certainly is and he'll be a good stud for a breeder interested in producing male slaves with exceptionally large pricks, always a major enhancement of a slave's sales price. This stud is most compliant, easy to arouse, and sexually tireless - you can breed him seven or eight times in a 24-hour period and find his fertility rate never falters and his interest never wanes, no matter who or what you put him to. He'll mate with the ugliest old hag you can imagine with no hesitation which makes him especially good for the breeder into utilizing cheap broods in their declining years - the type that have to fucked repeatedly to get pregnant anymore."

Three more pictures crossed the screen as João hit the "pause" button. [One showed a thin-waisted white boy with an exceptionally long prick fully hard; another showed an extremely muscular black proudly displaying his huge erection; and the third showed another white boy who looked like he was an embarrassed weight-lifter caught naked almost freakish with his long and very thick penis. All three looked like they were used to being displayed like this.]

"You may recognize two of these studs later in the tour because we are still using them in our rutting pens here. The other one, the handsome black stud, was sold during the past year as a personal sex slave to a young German master. It would be reasonable to assume the black is pleasuring his master by now, but it was our understanding his new owner, cognizant of his new property's value, is using his new purchase to breed new slave stock in his spare time utilizing his new master's wenches."

"We'll get to see the white Balkan slave with the real long prick," João interjected, "and the white American with the very thick prick in action when I get you down to the rutting sheds, Christian. I'm currently using both of these slaves for my own bed when I take a fancy to it and a female friend of my sister is using that thick pricked American stud every time she visits - she has him in her bed most every morning, afternoon, and night when she's around.

The narration continued: "The studs shown, like most studs nowadays, have been trained to show their big pricks hard anytime they are on display and all have learned to suck to the complete satisfaction of anyone they are assigned to. In addition, while on loan as pleasure slaves, they suffer a sore butt most all the time due to the number of people desiring to fuck them."

Again, João interjected. "I've been real happy with these studs in my own bed. You might enjoy using either or both of them some night while you're here. It's a real experience to fuck a slave whose main job is fucking wenches. You'd think they might resent it, but they seem to like the novelty of being fucked for a change. And, of course, if you appreciate size, these boys are in a class by themselves."

"Heard anything about the black stud since you sold him?" I asked.

"Well, yes, Christian. As a matter of fact, I ran into the slave and his master about a month ago at a country club I have guest privileges at in Berlin. He uses the boy as a 'display slave' when he's not serving as his chauffeur, so I saw him by his master at the club, standing beside him with his legs apart, his hands in back of his neck and his prick thrust out for all to see. He was being led around by a silver leash attached to the ring now fitted around his balls and the base of that big prick, but he also now sports large silver tit rings, and the tallest collar you've ever seen - a good 4" tall that forces his head into a chronic upright position that gives him a haughty look that's rather catching. You know how Germans like a disciplined look. But his new owner isn't stupid - he's renting the boy out for stud to anyone interesting in breeding their wenches. At least, when the boy isn't sucking or being fucked in his master's bed which is most of the time, I hear - at least until the novelty wears off!" João laughed.

"Sounds like he's getting his money's worth," Christian chuckled. "I'd pay plenty for a slave with a prick like that and I'm sure you had a good mark-up when you sold him to the German."

"Isn't that the whole point?" João laughed. "And eventually, I'm sure, when we sell off the other two studs shown in this presentation, the new owners of slaves like this will make sure those good slave genes aren't wasted. They'll be breeding again soon after we sell them off, I'll wager, even if their new owners aren't into breeding themselves when they realize how much those two will bring being rented out to the local rutting sheds."

João hit the "resume" button for the presentation and the narration continued.

"Studs are available in all skin colors but all offer desirable genetic traits: excellent musculature; high disease resistance; high endurance; high pain tolerance; strength; quick sexual response; high semen production; and quick sexual recovery following orgasm. Most studs are also selected for their attractive facial and body features although this trait isn't terribly important for the production of draft slaves, e.g., the mulatto stud shown previously is utilized exclusively for the production of common field slaves due to his rather common facial and bodily features. Studs don't sell unless they are well equipped for their assigned role. This reinforces their self-concept as a "born stud," leads to all other slaves and buyers viewing them as studs primarily (as opposed to draft workers, house slaves, etc.), and is used, rightly or wrongly, as one of the biggest elements in arriving at their sale price, e.g., the bigger the organs, the higher the price. [The screen displays an extremely handsome black posing to best show off his 12" circumcised shaft.] This prize stud is from Sierra Leone and was purchased for $380,000. Therefore, studs are usually shown fully erect (although not always as the American white slave shown previously was displayed flaccid - perhaps to emphasize the extreme breath of his organ) - and preferably with an 'interested' look in their eye as to their studding duties.

[The screen next shows a jet black slave displayed shackled by his hands and feet to a rutting bench where his large erect organ hangs beneath him.]

"Most studs placed in service are forced mated four to five times a day seven days a week and are expected to perform with whatever female brood is presented to them. They are not allowed any other sexual outlets, of course, in order to keep them focused on their primary responsibilities and are not allowed to talk to or otherwise communicate with the broods they are mated with to avoid any relationship issues. Most broods never even see the bucks put to them - they are usually blindfolded, chained face down on a bench which fully exposes their vagina and forces their legs wide apart. The stud takes her from the rear with his instrument fully greased so it can be fitted into smaller vaginas without damage. Once he has deposited a full load in the chosen brood, the overseer feels his balls to make sure he has completely emptied and then leads him back to his holding cell before the female is released and then later tested for impregnation. If she has not taken, she is taken back within her peak period for insemination by a different stud. This process is repeated until she is confirmed pregnant or her peak period of fertility is over for the month. If she has not been successfully impregnated, she is put back in her regular work assignment until her peak period of reception is again reached 24 days or so later. If she does not take after three months, she is sold off as infertile. If a stud's impregnation rate starts to drop, he is usually sold off as a mistress' or master's sex slave, to a male brothel, or as a display slave. If he is not unusually handsome, he is generally sold off as a common draft slave.

"Highly prolific studs sell from $100,000 up, dependent on overall looks, size of sexual organs, age, sexual endurance, and especially fertility rates. The stud shown here [the screen shows an extremely handsome slave] sold for $420,000 due to his age (only 22), skin color (brown), musculature, hit rate (60%), eager willing attitude, and extremely quick rate of full post-orgasmic recovery (he could be essentially bred six times a day if scheduled appropriately). At the low end of the scale, the rather common, but hugely equipped, mulatto stud shown previously sold for only $88,000 due to his age (34), skin color (mulatto), musculature (only fair), impregnation rate (down to 40%), and low rate of sexual recovery (he could now only be efficiently bred about twice a day). Still, the size of his organ kept his value up, even if only for a mistress' amusement at this stage in his life. The Balkan stud shown previously will be priced at $399,000 when he is sold off. His Balkan good looks, fine well honed and muscular bodybuild, his relative youth (still only 21) and his unusually huge organ all bring the price up. But his low "hit rate" (35%), his slow post-orgasmic recovery (up to three hours), and a surliness that requires whip management takes a good $100,000 to $200,000 off the price. The black slave shown on the screen now isn't phenomenally equipped, but his smooth black hide and good musculature will assure at least $300,000 at auction due to his youth, quick sexual response, and very high viable sperm count.

[The screen now shows one handsome white boy fucking another over a corral fence while a third white boy, equally handsome with a full hard-on waits his turn.]

"Today, however, huge numbers of slaves on the market were not born into their status, but come from many other sources. Those enslaved later in their lives can be purchased from all sorts of places. For example, this youth ranch in Texas, a state detention facility, regularly sells off its inmates to interested buyers. We bought all three of these boys for our own stock: the price was right; the boys are nice looking and properly trained for their new life as slaves; and they obviously take to being fucked without a shred of resentment.

[The next scene on the screen shows a young white master vigorously fucking a collared white slave about the same age.].

"Few male slaves are actually utilized as studs. Most slaves are purchased for the work to be extracted from their bodies. But, after a full days work, owners continue to utilize their slaves in the off-hours for their own amusement and pleasure. Every slave nowadays expects nothing less following some rigorous training and always strives to please their master or mistress no matter what is asked of them.

"In the future, however, it is clear more and more of the slave population will be products of breeding farms, almost all of whom already are practicing carefully controlled selective breeding procedures. Each new generation of slave products specifically bred for market will be a marked improvement over the last. Hence, every 18 years or so, we will notice significant advancement in musculature, disease resistance, body size, endurance and strength, not to mention overall attractiveness, size of sexual organs, sexual responsiveness, and even obedience. Within half a century, fourth generation slaves will be entering the market who will be, as a whole, remarkably handsome with most attractive muscular well-defined bodies, beautiful skin and hair texture, feature huge, remarkably responsive sex organs, and will be raised from birth to be totally subservient to whoever purchases them. In the interim, though, the marketplace offers plenty of bodies to choose from, most of whom were once free prior to be enslaved.

[The screen showed a tobacco brown slave boy holding his large erect prick in an inviting position with his muscular body posed to best display his attributes.]

"The slave shown on the screen now is actually a first generation slave and a former prisoner of the U.S. government, but he now does most of the estate's laundry, serves as a milk stud for his master's condiments, and pleasures his mistress on demand.

"Future slaves will require remarkably little training compared to that received by the boy shown on the screen. Indeed, most fourth generation slaves will seek out new ways to please their owners, present few discipline problems, and require little training in normal slave expectations for the home, i.e., pleasing their master or mistress in bed, serving and cleaning skills, gardening, cooking and laundry duties, etc. or for the estate, i.e., working to full capacity 12-14 hours in the fields at full capacity; hauling heavy loads, drayage with wagons and carts, heavy duty loading and unloading, etc. or even in the factories: 14 hour a day schedules chained to their assembly posts, consistent performance without heavy use or the whip or prods, and with a high regard for the quality of their output."

João hit the pause button and I thrust my prick deeper down the slave's throat and rested my beer on the quivering back of the black slave who had remained in place the entire time of the presentation despite João's constant kneading of his balls and dripping prick.

"It leaves a lot out, but I'll fill you in on that when we take a tour of the facilities here," João said.

I shot a full load well down the slave's gullet as his throat muscles massaged my entire shaft.

"Thank you, master," the slave said as soon as he had swallowed the entire load. "Shall I continue for a second round?" he inquired.

"Why not?" I responded and the slave once again swallowed the entire shaft and I felt his throat muscles once again as João punched the resume button on the DVD player.

CHAPTER 4

"This part will explain some about the present market in slaves," João said as lifted the two beers off of his 'table' and ordered the black slave to suck him.

"This black is too good sucking to waste as a piece of furniture," João laughed as the slave undid his fly and pulled João's substantial piece of meat out. Without hesitation, the black slave got to work as João carefully returned the beers to his back. "No reason he can't suck and be a table," João chuckled.

"This next part will give you some idea of where we sell slaves currently as well as who is buying them."

Again, the narration on the DVD resumed amidst the slurping sounds of two slaves sucking vigorously.

"Slaves are available in markets all over the world," the narrator began. "Prices vary with the invariable ebb of supply and demand, but have remained remarkably steady since the breeding farms went into full production, thereby assuring the steady increase in availability of slaves the world markets demand. About 60% of all slaves are now products of the breeding farms, the most productive of which are currently located in Brazil, most countries of Sub-Saharan Africa, Myanmar, South India, Saudi Arabia, eastern Poland, the Ukraine, Pakistan, Turkestan, and, just beginning production, the states of Mississippi, Texas, and Alabama in the United States in that order. But, of course, slave breeding is practiced world wide these days and, as far as is known, there is no country that doesn't have an operational slave breeding operation in production somewhere or other. Consequently, global markets can offer most anything a customer could possibly imagine and usually at a price they can afford."

"Some recent purchases from a huge breeding farm outside of Sao Paulo, Brazil illustrate the point. All were priced under $150,000 wholesale and all were guaranteed for a 90-day period.

[The screen showed one slave after another on display stands in every skin and eye and hair color imaginable, a huge variety of body sizes (although all were very muscular and firm), some with body hair, some without, males showing hard, and females usually pregnant. All shown were between 20 and 35 years of age and all looked like they were eager to find a new owner.]

"What is shown here is typical of breeding farm offerings, although most farms offer considerably more African and Asian stock. Brazilian farms, of course, like the country itself, produce racial mixtures, but this particular farm employs primarily white studs in an effort to "lighten the breed" which is obviously working in their case. Like shown, most slaves are presented to best display their bodily attributes when up for bid and most bred slaves like these are fully trained to meet any owner's expectations of their new purchase.

"The next largest sources of slaves (in descending order) is from capture (war booty or kidnapping), court adjudication due to some criminal activity, parental sale of children, or enslavement due to indebtedness. These newly enslaved generally need to be 'broken' to their new status, trained for extensive periods to perform their new duties with total submission and a willing acceptance without question of whatever is asked of them, and a dramatic change in self-concept to where they see themselves as nothing but property at the disposal of their owner.

"A lot of new stock ends up in lawyer's offices as a result of indebtedness or plea bargaining in a criminal offense. Lawyers then sell them to slave dealers on behalf of the court.

"Another source, especially with young adult and late teenage stock, are those caught selling drugs, especially in the United States. These boys have a quick trial, are sentenced to slavery, and are then often sold in small 'sheriff's sales,' perfectly legal in many Southern states of the U.S. and a major source of income for small counties and parishes in rural America as well as here in Brazil and most other South American countries.

"Others, especially those from third world countries, find themselves snatched by slave catchers who then sell in batch lots to slave wholesalers. Sub-Saharan Africa has turned into one huge harvesting ground for new slaves that cost their catchers little but the time and effort to round them up and cage them by the thousands. Other countries in considerable turmoil and instability (e.g. Iraq, Afghanistan, and Lebanon) are rife with mercenaries eager to line their pockets by selling off refugees they round up under gunpoint.

"Still other countries have a long tradition of slavery where the disenfranchised find themselves being sold off before they know it (e.g. Mauritania, the Sudan, Yemen and Chad).

"Some parents take a quick profit in selling an 'excess' child when credit card debt mounts or some special purchase, such as a new car or a nicer house, is desired. Children can be sold between the ages of 18 and 21, including the United States, without any special court order other than proof of age and some proof (such as a birth certificate) the child is theirs to sell. A good looking, well built late teenager can bring enough to add a luxurious game room to the house, pay for a new BMW, or pay off completely your American Express card.

[The screen showed an exceptionally handsome black-haired 18-year-old white boy with an athletic body and unusually large genitalia.]

"The boy shown here brought in enough at auction to pay for his two older brother's college tuitions, otherwise unaffordable to his parents."

"Wars are a great source of new meat for the market - even border skirmishes provide thousands of slaves for global markets each year. Captured soldiers are usually in the peak of their manhood, in good physical shape, and already trained to respond to heavy discipline. For most prisoners of war, their new life as a slave is little different from their life before since both are environments of heavy discipline and where all decisions are essentially made for them by others, whether it is the company commander or their new master. Nakedness is their new uniform; a slave collar is their new company badge; slave pens replace a barracks; and slave chow replaces K-rations. But otherwise life is remarkably similar."

[The screen showed four naked young men, all very attractive.]

"All of these boys chose the wrong side to be on, and, once enslaved, there will be no going back ever to their former 'free' status. However, these boys are lucky: they are all decent looking, three of the four have good muscular builds, and even the puny one has a boyish charm that ought to find him a decent owner. In this case, the chained boy ended up on a farm as a draft slave, the young boy ended up serving as a restaurant waiter available for sexual usage by any of the customers at any time, the boy in the middle ended up as a factory worker assembling autos 12 hours a day seven days a week and in his overseer's bed each and every night, and the heavy hung jock ended up as a slave athlete for the Liverpool Soccer Team and a rented stud when he wasn't playing. Overall, a decent outcome for any slave."

"Wherever they come from, and for whatever you want them for, slaves can be found to suit every preference.

[The screen showed an advertisement for very light skinned black slaves from an American dealer specializing in half-breed slaves.]

"This ad from an American slave house dealing only in half-breeds is a good example, i.e., mulattos, quadroons and octoroons. There are as easy to buy as lifting your phone. The two featured here were bred to order to assure practically hairless bodies, appealing good looks and large genital organs, but could have just as easily come through court sentencing, parental sale, or as war booty."

Again, João hit the delay button and stood up to stretch his legs. I noticed a fresh set of attending slaves entered the room and knelt near the wall with their knees wide apart to assure a proper display of their manhood.

I thrust my prick even deeper down the slave's throat that was currently servicing me and rested my beer on the quivering back of the black slave who had remained in place the entire time of the presentation despite Joáo's constant kneading of his balls and dripping prick.

"The DVD leaves a lot out, but I'll fill you in on that when the show's completely over," Joáo said.

I shot a full load well down the slave's gullet who was between my legs as his throat muscles massaged my entire shaft.

"Thank you, master," the handsome green-eyed slave said as soon as he had swallowed the entire load. "Shall I continue for a second round?" he inquired.

"Why not?" I responded and the slave once again swallowed the entire shaft and I felt his throat muscles once again go into action.

CHAPTER 5

"The next section sort of wraps it up," Joáo explained as he arched his back and discharged a heavy load down the black slave's throat. "You want to trade boys now? This black is just getting warmed up but I believe I'll like to compare him to that green-eyed boy you're slowly but surely filling up," Joáo chuckled.

The two slaves, their mouths stretched to the limit and with pricks clearly outlining their extended throats, never moved as their next assignment was being discussed. Their eyes were wide open, however, and sparkled as they tried to anticipate every nuance of their master's desires.

With that, we switched slaves and Joáo hit the resume button on the DVD player whereupon a magnificent piece of collared man-flesh filled the screen totally nude, fully erect, and with a huge smile on his face.

"One look at a handsome piece of slave flesh like that - ready and eager to please his master - justifies all the bother slavery puts us through," Joáo said.

"Yes, Joáo, if a body like that wasn't available for sexual use, it would be a crime against humanity," I laughed.

"Well, no worry, Christian. There are thousands out there on the market as good or better than the boy on the screen - all fully trained for our pleasure and all eager to earn their keep."

The DVD then showed a huge variety of slaves all posed in total nakedness; all collared and many tit-ringed; some genitally banded, some not; a few nose ringed; a few with rings dangling from their ears; some totally body shaved; some shaved below their necks; others hairy as a bear; others with only a light coating of hair naturally gracing their bodies; some with huge organs that defied probability; others normal; a few even smallish; some in their late teens; others as old as 50 or so, but most in the early twenties.

That finale brought the DVD to an end. It was only 30 minutes long but it did give the uneducated viewer, like myself, some idea of slavery in the world today. The two slaves attending us, having drained both of us twice during the show, were dismissed and the two new replacement slaves fetched us fresh drinks and promptly got on all fours to serve as our 'tables.'

"That's just part of the story, Christian," João picked up where he had left off. "Actually, slavery is no different now than it has ever been - it's basically no different than when the Romans were going strong except the world's a lot bigger now. The show didn't really cover thoroughly one of the largest potential sources of slaves - I guess it's just too obvious."

"What's that, João?" I asked, somewhat overwhelmed as this point.

"Breeding them," João responded. "The law is the same now as it was in 3000 B.C. and ever since - the product of a slave womb is a slave for life. In your country, Christian, they're just now getting into serious production, but some other countries are very advanced in this area - I understand here in Brazil we are breeding a good 80% of our slave stock now and Poland isn't far behind. I imagine in 20 to 30 years you'll have a good 60% of the slaves you see marketed coming from specialized breeding farms. I'm buying the first off of a farm in Mississippi specializing in production of big, handsome blacks. So far, they're everything they're hyping - big and muscular, a pretty brown color, handsome and well hung. Most importantly, they're fully acclimated to their slave status and don't need additional training like captive stock. You tell them to bend over and take a fuck - that's just what they do - instantly with no questions and with a big smile on their face because they're happy they can be of service. They cost a little more than the formerly free, but you save a lot of breaking and training costs. I'd recommend them when they become more available. The Romans had it down to an art once the war captives dried up so they never suffered supply problems and there is no reason we can't do the same, especially in the U.S. where demand will be so high."

"Of course, training is a lot more sophisticated now for the newly enslaved than in olden times. We don't have to beat them half to death to get them to accept their new lives without question. We've got a lot of drugs useful in breaking and training, much more effective training procedures, and a lot of control gadgets that make the whip almost, but not quite, obsolete - you know, electric prods for real memorable pain, detection implants to prevent any hope of running away, electrified dildos that can be worn everyday if necessary (like they use with almost all the slaves in the manufacturing plants nowadays), and anti-depressants to help the fragile ones through the first difficult days of adjustment. A good trainer can take the most rebellious wild slave you can think of and have him begging you to fuck him in no less than 60 to 90 days with the modern methods. More importantly, that training sticks through a lifetime - no need anymore to send them back for retraining or reminder sessions. Out of our last 1000 sales of slaves once free, we've only had two returned for retraining - that's why we can guarantee our stock with little risk."

"I haven't heard of any trouble with the slaves being introduced into New York and I know they're all former prisoners and such, at least to date. But I've read they get a lot of conditioning, as they call it, before they are put up for sale," Christian confirmed.

"The only slaves testing the limits, or beginning to backtalk, or hesitating in obeying an order - that sort of thing - are those who are captured, stripped down to the buff, branded, given a good whipping, and then put right up for auction. No serious training, no time to settle in to their new circumstances, nothing. Those are the ones you hear about acting up and where you have to take them back to the dealer or call the Slave Police, if you have them in your country. But pay a decent price at a reputable dealer and you don't have any of that - I don't care what your new properties were before they were enslaved - an Army general, a senator, a lawyer, a doctor

- anything. Proper training leads a slave to know that their old life is over once and for all and their new life is all that matters - serving whoever owns them with everything they've got - body and soul."

"I've had Eduardo, my main bed slave, for over six years now," João continued, "and never had anything but total compliance and he used to be the CEO of a major manufacturing company here in Brazil before he got caught embezzling funds and found himself enslaved."

"Frankly, João, I don't like any bed partner much over 25 or so, no matter how good he is," Christian said. "I didn't realize you liked older men. I guess I should be flattered you took up my invitation to visit my town house back in New York."

"What in the hell are you talking about, Christian? Oh!" João laughed, "I see where you're coming from. Eduardo's not old. He's still just 29. He was considered a boy wonder back in the business world. Of course, his career didn't last too long in that area - not nearly as long as it has as a sex slave. He was just 23 when I bought him."

"Well, in that case, I may ask to use him before I leave," Christian laughed. "For a moment there, I thought all you had hidden back in your bedroom was stock well past their prime and Niger and those attendants we just had servicing us were the exceptions arranged just for me."

"Christian, I do have some customers that like the older slaves for sex - they claim they feel more comfortable with a slave their own age."

"Well, each to their own. But I bet those slaves are still in great shape, can still get it up readily, and are still at least half-way decent to look at," I chuckled.

"Of course, Christian. I didn't say my customers were stupid."

"If they can afford the prices you charge for a piece of meat, no one is going to say they're stupid," Christian laughed. "By the way, I drive a dark brown Bentley. You don't happen to have a handsome slave in stock that is dark brown, do you? If so, he could drive my car and warm my bed. That way, I would be making a real statement: great design, the best features, perfection in action, and the combo just reeks class and good taste."

"I've got one that just came in with a coffee brown hide that's trained to perfection and is really something to look at. He'd fill the bill exactly," Joáo said in a tone that was pure salesmanship.

"How much?"

"For you, I'll discount it a little as long as you promise not to tell anyone I knocked a little off the price - hurts the dealership's image, you know if word got out you could wheel and deal with the stock's set prices. Five percent off and that's the absolute best I can do without losing on the slave. He cost me quite a bit."

"It's a deal," Christian said. "I assume we can get a slave property back to New York without too much hassle these days," I asked, unsure what the U.S. law was at this point on imported slaves.

"Well, there's an import fee charged by your government, greedy as it is. But you can ship them UPS these days without much trouble. If you take him with you, you'll have to figure in the airline tickets. If we ship him, it's on us," Joáo said professionally. "We can arrange everything for you if you want - he'll be delivered to your townhouse whenever you want with all the appropriate ownership papers, bills of sale, and custom receipts. We even insure them to make sure they arrive in good shape. To the U.S., that adds about $2000 delivery costs, so, with the five percent off, the stock you'd be buying would come to about $122,000, Christian. Somehow," he snickered, "I have a feeling that's pocket change to you."

"Jesus, Joáo, when it comes to selling slaves your mind works like a computer. How can you remember each slave's price, anyway?" Christian asked jokingly.

"That's my business, Christian," Joáo said with a wink. "What's the matter? Interested in a scrub slave for $16,000. I've probably got a few down in the back barns that have been traded in and I'd be glad to get rid of at least one of them before selling them off for body parts. One of them is a mulatto hung like a horse and you can tell he was a real looker back in his day. Traded in on some new stock by that plant producing Michelin tires over at Sao Paulo. That means he's had a plug up his ass from the tire factory for a number of years, but before that I understood he was once owned by a brothel in downtown Rio, so you know he was a real looker at one time and probably knows every trick in the book."

"Save it, João," Christian laughed. "I'm not in the market for a 50-year-old worn-out whore no matter how cheap the goods are. You forget I may be as rich as you are, my friend, and can do better than old clunkers."

"Well, I'll get a good $20,000 or so just selling his parts off," João said. "But you know me, a salesman at heart. Don't blame me for trying."

"I'm not criticizing anyone serving as my gracious host in Brazil," Christian laughed, "especially with a five percent discount."

"I'll have that beautiful brown boy ready for shipment anytime you want him when you get back to New York. And, if you want, you can try him out tonight in your own bed," João stated.

"I sort of had Niger in mind for tonight if your hospitality still holds," I sheepishly answered. "I sure enjoyed him last night."

"You can have both, you know, Christian," João laughed. "That is, if you're up to fucking both of them."

"You're going to wear me down to a nub, João," I laughed, "but I would like to see if the new slave is as well trained as you claim before shipping him all the way to New York."

"I'll have him delivered to your room about midnight. Surely by then, Niger will be ready for a little rest," João laughed. "He'll be delivered completely cleansed inside and out and fully greased up for a good fucking."

"How about later in the week, João? I think Niger will be enough for tonight."

"Oh, alright, Christian. I'll use him one last time tonight. He's a long way from being a virgin anyway,' João laughed. "In the interim, let's go back to the manor house for a good lunch and then I can show you some of my house staff. We need to do that before we begin a tour of the main facilities here."

Christian gave a quizzical look at João, glancing at the two slaves in the room.

"Oh, all right. You can fuck my attendant while I fuck yours," João said. "Seems fair enough, but I must warn you, Christian. I'm about fucked out for today. You Americans never seem to wear out, despite all the talk about machismo here in Brazil."

Soon, João had exhausted my attendant slave to his complete satisfaction and I had explored all aspects of João's attendant. After that, the two slaves were ordered to douche and then shower and we proceeded to the main house.

When we got back to the manor house, João showed me three of the best pieces of male flesh I had ever seen, part of his house staff. The first slave's skin was a very smooth cream color with no blemishes whatsoever. His body was well defined, but not overly muscular like a weight-lifter's might be. His face was almost feminine it was so beautiful with fine black ringlets framing the face highlighted by a jet black pencil line beard outlining his jaw-line. He had flashing jet black eyes, prominent ringed brown nipples, beautifully sculpted pecs and abs, and a long, thick, circumcised penis at good 10" long atop balls the size of a couple of peaches. His body was totally hairless below his neck, which made his gold collar, tit rings, and thick genital band display beautifully.

"This slave is even better in bed than he looks like he might be," João explained as he stroked the slave to a full erection until the boy was dripping heavily.

The second slave presented was a pure black trimmed with a gold collar, gold genital band, and gold tit rings.

"This is the slave I mentioned before - he's one of the first out of the Mississippi breeding farm I was talking about before," João explained as he rubbed the black's slave muscular butt appreciatively.

The slave was so sexy that I got all hot again and could barely pay attention to João's third presentation, a muscular boy with sandy brown hair, a light dusting of body hair he was allowed to keep, a cute face, and a phenomenal prick fully erect between his two widely-parted legs.

"Another American boy," João explained as he hefted the slave's balls and bounced them around in the palm of his hand possessively. "Part of a large lot of slaves sold by the Texas prison system to a big dealer in Rio. When I saw him, I just had to have him for some reason or another."

"I think I can understand your need to buy him," Christian said as he ran his hands over the slave's sculptured pecs and twisted his tit rings a little.

"You know when I bought him, I took him with me, right out of his holding pen, to my hotel room in Rio and spent the next two hours fucking him slowly and thoroughly even though it wasn't even noon yet," Joáo chuckled. "And you know what he said to me when I was through plowing his ass, Christian?"

"I'm surprised he could say anything after that, Joáo," I laughed.

"The slave here said, 'Thank you, master,' when I dismissed him from my bed at long last. And then, Christian," Joáo continued, "with a worried look on his handsome face, he ventured, 'Was I as pleasing as Master's other bed slaves?'"

"Christian, I told him: 'Why, you horny bastard. What's the matter? Getting jealous of your competition? But then I told him he was fine - I just thought he was a little too tight in the ass, but I'd take care of that over time.'"

"You know, Christian, this slave looked relieved and a smile crept across his face. I guess he thought he wouldn't be traded in right away, at least. And you're still here, aren't you, slave?" Joáo asked the handsome American boy.

"Yes, master," the beautiful piece of man-flesh responded with a big smile on his face. "Would master or his friend like to use me now, master?" he ventured.

"Hold your horses, boy. All in due time," Joáo laughed as he continued kneading the boy's balls.

CHAPTER 6

That night, Joáo had Niger in my room as I'd requested and when I arrived after a pleasant evening visiting with Joáo, the black slave was on his knees beside my bed, his head bowed as far as his heavy metal collar would allow, with his knees spread wide. As usual, somehow he was fully erect and, head still bowed, he informed me he had shaved (actually he had little body hair anyway), showered, given himself a series of enemas so he was totally cleaned out, and greased his chute. As I looked his body over in all its naked glory, knowing he was totally at my disposal, I couldn't help but become aroused myself.

"Niger, you said you were from Mississippi," I stated as I began to peel off my clothes and let them drop to the floor. "How in the hell did you end up here?"

"Yes, master, I'm from Hattiesburg, Mississippi originally" Niger replied. "But when I was 18, I got busted for selling drugs down in the projects and ended up in the sheriff's detention center a few miles out of town. There were hundreds of us down there, kept in sort of a stockade way back in the woods with big electrified fences. Most of us were young, mostly black but not all, and pretty defenseless since we were kept shackled all the time with our arms locked behind our backs and our feet chained so we couldn't step more than 8" or so. Since we were more or less out of sight, the sheriff had us stripped - claimed we wouldn't run when we were as naked as we were born. At first we tried to act tough but that's kind of hard when you're buck naked and chained up like a trussed pig. But within a week, we were taken one-by-one into a small 'interrogation' room and strapped down to a saw horse where the sheriff's guards and some of his long-term 'trustees' raped us over and over no matter how hard we screamed or tried to get loose. These 'interrogations' went on every day after that until it didn't hurt so bad and we gave up screaming but just thought of it as part of the living hell of the place. Eventually, we just laid down on that saw horse when they took us to the room and let them strap us down without anyone having to whip the crap out of us or knock us senseless when we resisted. After that, we had to thank the bastards for fucking us when they had finished with us or we got the bejesus whipped out of us. We knew everyone was getting 'the treatment' as they called it, so it wasn't as if we were being singled out or anything. Furthermore, since everyone was getting fucked regularly, we never thought of ourselves as 'deviant' or 'queer.' It was just what we had to do to stay alive. But, master, we were the house whores and we knew it."

"Was that your introduction to sex, Niger?" I asked.

"No, master. Before I was busted I was always fucking some cunt from the projects since I had been 13 or 14 - can't remember, master. Sometimes some really cute little snatches would trade a good fuck for a fix. But me being the one getting fucked was all new to me and most of the other boys until I got to the Sheriff's detention center. But we got use to taking it up the ass within a month or so and then we had to learn to suck which wasn't too hard when you were a whore anyway. They speeded the whole process up by not letting us getting off ourselves unless they gave permission and the only way they gave that was when you sucked them off particularly well or gave them a good fuck up your ass. After a week or so of not shooting off, you'll do most anything to get a little relief. At least, that was true for me, master, and most of the other boys at the center back in Mississippi. We were just teenagers and used to having our balls drained regularly, Master."

"Once we were fully 'trained' as they put it and were used to parading around naked all the time, one day the sheriff himself had us all lined up, still in chains, and a fleet of real fancy cars arrived on the other side of the fence. Some smartly dressed men and women got out of those limousines, came through the gate, and started down the line of us, feeling us all over, checking out our muscles, looking at our teeth, fondling our pricks until we all got hard, and ordering us to bend over while they stuck their fingers up our holes and wiggled them around to see how tight we were back there. We are all embarrassed to death - especially with women pawing over us like this - but the sheriff's guards really laid into you with a whip if you objected at all and, if that didn't stop you squirming around while the hands roamed all over you, they used their electric prods which about knocked you out it hurt so bad.

"Did they tell you anything about what was going on?" I asked, now fully naked myself and relaxing on the bed.

"No, master. They never told us anything - why they were fucking us every day, who these fancy dressed people were, when we would get out of there, nothing like that, master."

"Well, they looked you over and then what, Niger?" I asked.

"Those of us that were young and good looking and well hung were sorted out first, master, and taken to a big hall there at the retention center where we really got looked over - they stroked us to erection, jerked us off, put big dildos up our asses, kneaded our nipples until they got all swollen and erect, that sort of thing. I felt like a mule up for auction, master, except I don't know of any mule getting sold having things shoved up its ass or getting jerked off right there in public. Then one by one, the sheriff auctioned us off like cattle and I got 'bought' by some strange looking man that turned out to be an agent for Master de Silva. Of course, back then, I still didn't understand what was going on and the idea of being sold off as property was beyond me. You see, master, I didn't know about slavery then - it was just getting started in the States back then and I had always thought that ended with the Civil War, Master."

"What happened to those who weren't so pretty?" I asked.

"Oh, I understood they got taken to another building and the same thing happened except no one cared about how they looked or how sexy they were - they were just interested in their muscles and how much work they could get out of them. I learned later they were all sold off as draft slaves for the farms and factories, Master."

"That's where the bulk of slaves end up," I commented. "What happened once you were sold to the de Silva agent, Niger?"

"He bought eight of us at that sale, Master, and the Sheriff then had the eight of us taken down to the welding shop there at the detention center and had a iron collar welded around our neck and a big iron band welded around our equipment so our sex was forced out for a full display at all times. They left our shackles on. After that, the Sheriff had the eight of us delivered to an airstrip not too far away and we got herded into a big cage built inside one of Master de Silva's airplanes where there were two slave handlers on board with whips to keep us in line and water us. The agent stayed in Mississippi with the Sheriff and I've only seen him once or twice since then when I have been sent to his room here on the ranch for his enjoyment of me. After the long flight where I had fallen asleep but woke up hungry as hell, the eight of us were here at the ranch and I've never been off it since except when I'm driving the master's car."

"They must have trained you," I commented, 'in view of what you do now."

Niger blushed, turning his black skin purple.

"You mean being a sex slave?" Niger asked.

"Well, something like that," I said as I began to play with myself lying on the bed, finding the conversation very erotic.

"Yes, master. All eight of us joined about 60 other new slaves being trained for the sex market. We eight were all black Mississippi boys, but the others were from every country in the world - places I'd never heard of - and were about every color too. None of us spoke Portuguese back then and it was hard to communicate with each other, but I soon learned the white boys were from Poland, Slovakia, Rumania, Russia, and the United States and Australia. But they had boys there from India, Thailand, Malaysia, Samoa, and Mexico along with guys as black as I am from central Africa and some big brown boys from Senegal and Mauritania. What we had in common was we were all 'pretty' boys as they called us, we were all hung like horses, and we were all young and vigorous."

"You know, master, back in the projects we black boys thought no one was hung better than Mississippi black bucks. But when we saw our new training partners, a lot of them made us look downright puny," Niger giggled.

"The trainers here taught us to understand what we were now - slaves - just owned property; that we were being trained for resale as sex slaves who would follow any command without question in return for being housed and fed; and any objections to all of that would be meet with a quick trip to the whipmaster for a memorable lesson in what happens to slaves when they don't do exactly what they're told without question; and that essentially we were to provide any pleasure our pretty bodies could offer whoever bought us. The alternative was being sent to the rendering plant, located right here at the estate, or sold off to the emerald mines where, if lucky, we might last six months under the whips.

"When we lost our appeal, we would be sold off again in all likelihood, probably as draft slaves for the plantations or factories in whatever country we were in at the time and, after the last ounce of work left in our bodies had been extracted there, we would be sent, like all slaves eventually, to the rendering plants so our still functioning organs could be harvested, our hides could be tanned, and the rest of us turned into protein concentrate, one of the main ingredients in the special dry chow now fed to slaves around the world. So it was in our best interest to keep our bodies in perfect shape, our sexual skills honed, and our attitudes eager and willing at all times."

"Wow! Those trainers lay it on straight, don't they, Niger?" I chuckled.

"Yes, master. The scenario was motivational. When I understood that's exactly what a slave's world was like, I decided then and there I better make the most of it and do what they said."

"But it wasn't that easy, was it, Niger?" I prompted.

"No, master. Despite my good intentions, a slave has to be 'broken' to his master's will, just like they say and that takes a lot of pain, hunger, feelings of helplessness, and despair. After a session under the bull whip, after you have to earn every scrap of food, water, and sleep through doing exactly what they say without question, after having to earn sexual relief yourself through pleasing your master completely, and after learning thoroughly you no longer own your body or determine what you do or have any choices in this world other than doing what your master or mistress says - only after a long period of this do you turn into a proper slave. That's mainly what training is all about, Master. Of course, we were fucked continually, had pricks thrust down our gullets on a regular basis, fucked a cunt or another man's ass on command at least every other day, got used to having our tits and our pricks played with - that too teaches you you're just owned property now as well as teaches you what your function is in life. The big change comes when you realize you are nothing but a slave and always will be - the property of whoever buys you. But that change happens eventually and the trainers are experienced enough to know when you've settled into being a slave. At that point, you're 'broken' as they call it. That's when they sell you off to a new home."

"But you're still here, Niger," I noted.

"Yes, master. Along with Thor and a couple of brown slaves and a white American boy the Master wanted for himself. So we haven't been sold off yet, Master."

"Interesting, Niger, but it's time you got to work," as I indicated I wanted him to suck my organ, hard as a rock by now.

Niger smiled and climbed up on the bed, swallowing my entire length in one gulp before massaging me with his throat muscles. Just before I exploded into his mouth, I withdrew, had him roll over onto his back and then fucked him deeply once his muscular legs were up over my shoulders.

When I had deposited a full load well up his rectum, I told Niger to flush out. When Niger got off the bed to comply with my command, I noticed another slave was now kneeling beside the bed - a well muscled blond I quickly recognized as the stud Thor.

"What are you doing here, slave" I asked.

"My master thought you might want to use me tonight, master," Thor replied with his eyes lowered.

"Well, Niger has pretty well drained me right now, but perhaps a little later," I replied. "But Niger told me you were trained here at the same time he was. What's your story?" I asked.

"Master? What do you mean?" Thor responded.

"Where did you come from, Thor, and how did you end up a stud slave here in Brazil. You don't look like you were born here," I answered.

"Oh, I understand, Master," Thor replied humbly. "Master bought me from an Argentine prison when I was nineteen, Master. Most prisoners in Argentina are sold as slaves nowadays, Master, in that the government likes the money they get out of it and they don't have to feed and house us once we're sold, so it makes sense. I was shipped up here to the ranch and placed into training along with, as he said, Niger and all the others. We had a large group being trained at the same time, although the groups now are even larger, Master. After we were completely trained as sex slaves, Master looked us all over to decide who he wanted to keep here at the ranch and who he wanted to sell off at the next auction. As Niger may have told you, Master, he and I, two brown boys and an American white were all chosen to stay here as Master's own sex slaves. But Master decided I was to serve stud as well, Master, and I've been sent down to the rutting sheds almost every night since then. Master says I've sired over a thousand new slave pups already he can sell off once they're full grown and I imagine they're all different colors and sizes since I've been put to about every type of breeding wench imaginable."

"You like studding?" I asked since I found the role of a human stud unimaginable.

"No, master," Thor answered without hesitation, "but I have no choice as a slave."

"No, you don't, Thor," I agreed. "But a lot of free men I know claim they would like nothing better than being a stud."

"Yes, master. When I was 16 back in the barrios, I talked like that too, but making new slaves with slave women you never know - you're simply told to mount them and fuck - it's different. Normally, the broods are blindfolded so they don't know who is fucking them and we only see their backsides since they are shackled to the rutting benches. That's a long way from 'making love' as I thought of it when I was fucking my girlfriend back in Argentina. Studding is just a chore here no different than shoveling coal or hacking the sugar cane."

"Oh, get off it, Thor. You don't have a nice little orgasm out in the cane fields."

"No, master. That's nice, but it's still a job."

"I suppose when you're primarily a stud, you don't look too forward to getting fucked by the master or- like me - one of his guests," I chuckled.

"No, master, I hate getting fucked or having to suck someone off," Thor answered, again totally honestly.

"Really?" I asked. "I thought Master de Silva fucked you on a regular basis."

"He does, Master. He says he enjoys fucking a slave that deeply resents it but knows he can't do a damn thing about it," Thor said so unemotionally that you would think we were talking about the weather.

"You mean you're not going to enjoy it when I fuck the shit out of you tonight, slave?" I asked, rather irritated with his honesty.

"No master, I'll hate it in that I don't like being used by another man and never did - just not built that way I guess - but that doesn't mean you'll be disappointed with me, Master. I can take a fuck with the best of them and bring you real pleasure, Master. That's what I have to do, Master, - bring you all the pleasure my body is capable of - and, as a slave, that's what I'll do. Master, what a slave may feel about use of his body doesn't have anything to do with your use of that body. No one cares what a slave feels or thinks about anything, Master. You learn that real quickly in your slave training, Master. In fact, Master, Master de Silva really only likes to bed down bucks that resent it. He claims it makes for a better fuck."

"Is he right, Thor?" I asked.

"I don't know, Master. The only thing I ever fuck are breeding wenches."

"Somewhere down the line, Thor, they'll pull you off of studding. What then?" I asked.

"If I'm lucky, they'll sell me off to a mistress or master looking for a personal sex slave who has a lot of experience and fully understands their role as a slave. If I'm not so lucky, they'll sell me off to a factory where I'll be chained to a work station with a electrified dildo up my butt to make sure I work as hard as I can 12 to 14 hours a day. If I'm really unlucky, I'll end up sold off to the mines where I end up in a rendering plant within six months or so if the stories I hear are half-way true."

"Sort of a bleak scenario, Thor," I commented. "Wish you were back in that prison?"

"No, Master," was the quick reply.

"Why not?" I asked.

"You tend to never get released from Argentine prisons unless you're sold off - everyone knows that. And while you're in prison, everyone fucks you that can still get it up if you're even half-way decent looking. I got fucked more there than I ever have as a slave, including during training, Master. And at least the people fucking me here are decent looking. Besides, the food's a lot better, the accommodations are nicer here, and prison is as confining as being a slave - either place you don't decide what's going to happen to you or what you will be doing. No, master, I'm a lot better off being kept naked all the time with a collar around my neck, rings through my tits, and with my manly equipment all banded so it shows off properly. Slaves are worth a lot of money, Master, and owners tend to take care of their expensive property."

"A healthy perspective if I do say so, Thor," I complimented the slave as I motioned for him to get on all fours so I could mount him now that I had properly recovered from Niger's efforts.

Without hesitation, Thor assumed the commanded position with his knees spread wide apart to allow full access to his greased hole. As I climbed on him, I grabbed his ringed tits and shoved my prick deeply up his chute. He moaned in a slave's acceptance of his servitude.

CHAPTER 7

The next morning, Joáo was eager to show me his entire facility. I was well rested since once I finished with Thor, I went promptly to sleep and never woke up until I smelled the coffee drifting into my bedroom where both Thor and Niger were asleep on floor.

Joáo looked to be just as rested, explaining he had retired early with the well-trained slave he had sold me yesterday as well as the two brown boys he kept around as favored sex slaves but they had drained him completely by 10 o'clock and he had lost interest in their bodies after that.

After a quick but delicious breakfast of scrambled eggs, crisp bacon, orange juice, and some of those specially frosted cinnamon rolls we both liked so well, we headed out in two rickshaws both pulled by naked dray slaves in full harness.

"Did you like those scrambled eggs?" Joáo asked, yelling over from the other rickshaw.

"They were delicious," I yelled back.

"Yes. The secret is mixing the eggs with cream and fresh cum before cooking them," Joáo yelled back. "It's the only way I like eggs anymore."

"That poor black slave in the kitchen gets pumped once again," I laughed.

Within minutes, we reached our first destination, the muscular slaves pulling us now drenched with sweat but breathing easily.

"This is the processing center for new slaves," Joáo said as he led the way into a huge warehouse with numerous rooms branching off from the main arena. "We're processing a batch that just came in on last night's flight from a big market in Senegal, so you'll get to see what we do to a new purchase to get them started out right."

Lined up 60 long, the slaves were first being given an enema, then showered, then body shaved, then collared, and finally led to a medical examination station where blood, urine, and semen samples were all collected, musculature and bone structure was assessed, and genitals were measured both flaccid and erect, circumcisions were performed on those needing it, and balls were kneaded and weighed before genital rings were welded into place. They were then moved to a station where their tits were pierced, their butts were branded with the de Silva ownership mark, and a GPS location device was embedded deep up their rectum where no one could ever remove it. At the next station, a bar code was tattooed onto the outside of their right arm so it would be easy to identify them the rest of their lives. Any objections to all of this were met with quick, instantaneous use of the electric prods. After an application or two, most of the new slaves never said another word or hesitated in meeting any command outside of the raw screams that the branding and tit-piecing usually produced. Most were, of course, reduced to tears through shame, humiliation and pain, but no one paid the slightest attention to it. Finally, an 'evaluation' team assessed each prepared slave individually and he was classified as to his future training, i.e., drayage, field work, factory work, house slave, personal service slave, etc., although all would receive 'basic' training in instant response to commands in both Portuguese and English, proper display positions, sex usage, personal hygiene, keeping their body in top shape through proper diet and exercise, and identifying symptoms of common slave diseases which needed to be reported to their handler at the appropriate time. The latter two were emphasized as responsibilities of a slave to protect their master's investment in their body and any negligence in this area, like suicide or self-destructive behavior, was seen as a crime against their master, no different than theft - a charge leading to severe consequences for any slave property.

Once general job classifications were decided, slaves had their hair trimmed and/or shaved appropriate for their chosen occupation and appropriate exercise and diet programs were individually prescribed to best enhance the investment.

"Basically, it's fairly simple," Joáo said. "Now we're off to the training facilities so you can see what happens to a slave next. I can't show you all of them - we have a separate facility for each general occupation, but I can show you the one they all go to first - the 'basic' training."

What Joáo showed me there was harsh, but obviously necessary, although previously owned slaves or bred slaves were waived from this training, it obviously not being necessary. The training started with learning through doing the required positions slaves needed to know: proper kneeling, full display, kneeling display, "at ease," obeisance, etc. It wasn't much different than basic Army training except for the emphasis on proper display of the naked body. Next was command response training in both English and Portuguese; next was 'voice control', e.g. learning to only speak when asked a direct question other than "Yes, Master," "No, Master," "I don't know, Master," "Right away, Master," etc., and who was to be addressed as "Master" and who was to be addressed as "Sir." Also was instruction in how to thank a master for disciplining them, for sexual use of their body, etc. During this stage, the slave lash was used at the slightest hesitation or mistake and repeated mistakes lead to use of the bull whip where lessons learned were invariably permanent at the risk of body scarring. Consequently, the electric prod applied directly to the balls was obviously substituted for this last stage of discipline with about the same results: a permanent change of behavior and attitude. Occasionally, none of these methods seemed to take hold. Then, food deprivation, water deprivation, and sleep deprivation in that order were utilized and invariably worked. There were no martyr slaves in the final analysis!

"This is all pretty common-sense," Joáo said as screams and moans of instant punishment filled the air along with wild looks of total despair and beseeching looks toward Joáo and I to intervene which we fully ignored, of course. The trainers Joáo utilized were good at their work and didn't let anything interfere with 'breaking' the slaves to their new lives. Joáo pointed out they believed harshness up front led in the long run to a happier slave and the facts bore them out, although the trainees couldn't see this at this point in their new life obviously. There was never a question as to whether the methods utilized would work. Everyone knew they worked extremely well universally with anything purchased, no matter what that's slave's previous life as a freeman had been like or where they had been obtained.

Next on Joáo's tour was one of the 'specialized' training centers, in this case a center for training 'personal service slaves' where the rickshaws took us at a brisk pace, the slaves pulling us again working up a good sweat in the process.

The place was filled with only the best slaves available in terms of good looks, nice appealing bodies, and all were amply equipped to please most anyone. Most were in their very late teens or early twenties, although not all. Most were muscular, well sculptured, and obviously proud of their bodies. Most had extremely handsome faces and exuded a sexual magnetism that only a few slaves seemed to possess. When we entered, the place reeked of animal heat, semen, and old-fashioned body sweat. Some were mounted on benches being fucked by the trainers, others were on their knees taking the trainer's huge cocks down their throats, still others were fucking female slaves under the heavy eye of a trainer holding a whip, a few were fucking each other under another trainer's ever-ready whip, and still others were standing with their legs spread wide apart, their banded genitals thrust out as far as possible while trainers were "milking" them into small cups which were then passed on to other trainees to drink down in a single gulp. Everywhere one could hear the sounds of gagging and choking as new trainees learned to stretch their throats; slaves gasping in the process of orgasming as they were being sucked off, milked, or fucking; the slurping and munching sounds of experienced cock suckers; and the deep groans (and a few retching screams) of those new to taking a huge cock up their ass.

"A few weeks of this and you're good for anyone's bed," João chuckled. "The best thing is, no matter what experiences the slaves have had before in this area - and it's mainly been just fucking their girlfriends or former wives - they learn to like it after a time. The trainers tell me it's because slaves learn a good fucking can be pleasurable once you get used to it, a load of fresh cum tastes good compared with the monotony of slave chow, and fucking on command, like a mistress demands, beats not fucking at all. I think they learn to like it because all slaves crave human contact and this, while no substitute for a relationship with a person you love, is certainly better than no contact at all which is the alternative. You've got to remember, Christian, a slave can't even beat off unless his master or mistress allows it. So this is a hell of a lot better than being 'blue-balled', i.e, forced to sit there with a dripping erect prick and swollen balls a good deal of the time. Of course, the gay boys take to man sex with a vengeance - they're in slave heaven so to speak, but the same could be said for the straight boys sold to a mistress even though they certainly can't just hump and dump like they used to probably."

"Do you sell gay slaves to gay men and straights to the mistresses, then, João?" I asked.

"Hell no, Christian. Why would we limit ourselves like that? Slaves do what they're told and it doesn't matter one iota what their natural inclinations are. That's why we train them! No one gives a shit about a slave's natural bent anyway. They do what they're told to do and that's that."

"I get the picture," I replied meekly, sorry I've even bought up such a stupid question.

"Once they're trained for whatever we have in mind for them - the mines, the factories, the farms, the bedroom, the brothels, whatever - we prepare them for final sales. I'll show you the holding pens and auction room next if you're not bored with all of this," João announced.

"Hardly bored, João. Fascinated is a better word. Again, I'm so naive in this area I feel like I'm seeing an alternate planet or something. Lead on, if you don't mind, but I would like to see another special training facility if we could. The sex training is interesting, but most slaves are probably sold for labor than sex."

"You're not so naive after all, Christian," João laughed. "You're dead right on that. After all, being a personal service slave is really only a possibility for the exceptionally good looking and well hung. Most slaves don't qualify and they end up being bought for how much work can be extracted from their bodies with the least amount of trouble extracting that work."

With that, we jumped back in the rickshaw awaiting us outside and were quickly taken to another facility at a fast trot. This facility was a mile or so away and the slaves were breathing hard by the time we got there, again coated with sweat. There had been an incline the whole way but the slaves never slowed down although both of them were gasping for air by the time we got there.

This facility was outdoors and I witnessed some slaves swinging heavy picks under a constant barrage of whips landing on their backs and rumps any time they slowed the pace. Other slaves were in full harness pulling heavily laden wagons while a driver lashed out at their backs and rumps with a long reaching 'cat of nine tails' whenever they slowed in the slightest. Some slaves were hitched to a plow while their overseer used an electric prod on them whenever it seemed they weren't pulling with full effort. All these slaves were unshaven, had only the rain to wash them, and obviously weren't allowed breaks for their bodily functions - shit was dried on their legs and they just pissed in place. Some already had backs scarred and bleeding. Most had head hair matted with filth. The stench from their bodies wafted up to any observers, including ourselves.

"No one buys slaves like this for their looks," João said without apology. "What's important with these slaves' bodies is strength, endurance, and disease resistance. What we teach them here is to always perform up to their maximum, ignore the pain of their exhaustion (through heavy discipline that prevents any natural slowdowns), and that any resistance is futile. They learn these things amazingly fast and by the time we market them as draft slaves, they're damn good workers - well worth the money they cost. I guarantee you, Christian," João boasted, "these slaves are the cheapest form of labor you can ever come across - hell, they're cheaper than any mechanization that's on the market. Four slaves on a plow is a hell of a lot cheaper, both in original cost as well as maintenance, than the cheapest tractor being sold today and will last just about as long if you pay attention to their feed."

"I imagine that has a lot to do with the popularity of slaves around the world," I ventured.

"Economically, it's the only way to go if you want to remain competitive in most enterprises today, including mining, farming, manning factories - the whole gamut where labor is a major component of the final product.

"Well, I can't take this stench too much longer," I laughed. "I've seen enough here for today. But can we still take in your holding pens and auction facility?"

We quickly returned to the rickshaws where our pullers were silently reminiscing on their own training in this very facility. For some reason, the slave pulling my rickshaw had a huge erection which he couldn't touch since his hands were shackled to the poles of the rickshaw. I supposed he had been denied any sexual relief for some time and it was beginning to show. When I asked João about this, he said I was right, but denying a slave any sexual relief often led to a greater work output and most owners made it a practice nowadays, although the downside was seeing a lot of dripping erect pricks among the draft slaves like those in front of us.

João must have been right, because without any urging from the whip, the slaves ran at full speed to our destination, a good two miles away, well aware they would face cut rations that night if they didn't as João pointed out while we were zooming along.

"João, is the slave's good performance due to the sex restrictions or the threat of cut rations?" I yelled over to him as we were jostled along.

"Who cares, Christian. It may be a combination of both. The important thing is in their performance."

Within 12 minutes we were at the sales center, as João called it. First we viewed the holding pens. There were hundreds of small cages lining the walls where the slaves up for sale could easily be viewed. They were so small a slave was practically jammed against one set of barred sides or another so anyone had access to all parts of their body in order to inspect them. Of course, most buyers preferred to view them out in front of their cages and all slaves were used to this - upon command they crawled out of their cages and presented themselves in full display position (hands in back of their neck collar, legs spread wide apart, and their pelvis and chest thrust forward) in front of any potential buyer. As we visited, about 12 slaves were out in front of their cages being pawed and fondled in a full inspection. Another 10 or so were being looked at within their cages by those just browsing the whole lot of them.

João had most everything available in those holding pens anyone could want - everything from the beautiful pleasure slave to breeding wenches to brutish looking masses of muscles mainly useful in the mines. There was every color and every nationality although the slight majority of his stock was Brazilian of course.

The sales room was basically a theater - a stage with full display lighting with plush individual seating out front for the comfort of the buyers. This place was the only place we had visited so far that was air-conditioned. Where slaves were processed, classified and trained were all steamy and hot, so I wasn't surprised the slaves up on the stage, despite the hot lighting, were shivering a bit in their complete nakedness.

"Do sales go on continually, João?" I asked in amazement that a slave auction was taking place as we were visiting during the early afternoon.

"This is a big operation. We generally have sales going on up until about midnight and starting around 10 in the morning. That way a buyer can shop whenever he likes. Some of the smaller places have scheduled auctions like once a week or so, but that's where our sheer volume can do them in every time. Convenience sells, Christian, as you can see for yourself."

Indeed, I could see. There were about 20 or so in the audience, and a good five of them were in heated competition to buy a huge black draft slave that was ugly as sin but a mass of muscles. The slave looked to be no more than 19 so there were probably decades of good hard work left in him. While we watched, he sold for $98,000 to a Japanese man.

"He got a good buy," João commented. "About right for a good draft slave."

Next on the stage was a handsome American boy about 20 or 21 with a nice build, a very light brown skin, blue eyes, a large, thick neatly circumcised prick and black hair. He was being sold as a 'house slave' and brought $231,000 within minutes.

Joáo studied the buyer, a huge black man, and chortled. "That boy's been bought by Senor Alcatrar who owns a string of brothels in most of the major Brazilian cities. Senor Alcatrar will get his money back on that boy within five years and still can sell him for $75,000 pure profit as a labor slave. Of course, by then, the boy's washed up sexually, but it won't matter as a labor slave. That's how you get rich, Christian. As I said, listen and learn!"

CHAPTER 8

THREE YEARS LATER:

Joáo had been dead right about America's reaction to the availability of slaves. Markets across the U.S. were now flooded with slaves as the government busily offered its entire prison population, emptied the jails, cleared out the rehab centers, and swept up the unemployed - all now offered at public auction to anyone with the wherewithal and the inclination to add human livestock to their home or business.

Everywhere you went you saw slaves in action - so much so, you wondered who did all the work before slavery. They now harvested your food, manned your office, dug the coal and iron ore, built the roads, did most of the construction, filled the labor needs of almost all industrial and manufacturing plants, took over most security posts, quarried the stone and marble, washed the cars, staffed the cattle ranches, did most of the logging, handled all the gardening chores, crewed your yacht, did almost all agricultural chores, drove the trucks and buses, chauffeured the cars, and even cleaned your pools. Not to mention all the dirty work: sewage workers, septic tank cleaners, garbage collectors, landfill workers, etc. The United States, just like João's Brazil and most other countries in the world, had embraced the re-institution of slavery with a passion, so much so it was hard to imagine how America had managed before.

At any rate, the bulk of America's work was now being done cheaply, efficiently, and well. After all, there were no wages or fringe benefits to be paid and slaves were cheap enough to buy due to the huge supply. Efficiency was obtained with a good overseer who wasn't afraid to use the whip and the electric prods as needed. Food was nothing more than the cheap slave chow that had been developed; clothing was nothing more than a collar, some body fittings, and a few rags for outdoor slaves in the winter; and shelter was as simple as a cellblock with a few bunks and a shower if you were fancy and a blanket for sleeping on the floor and a bucket if you wanted to cut costs to the bone. Quality work was assured through keeping slaves sex-deprived all the time and then granting sex relief as a work privilege; access to extra portions of slave chow or a rest break occasionally, and, if that didn't work, branding, the bull whip, and electric prods were great motivators that seemed to work universally well with most any slave, no matter what his background or temperament.

Christian thought that he could have predicted as much himself. He remembered three years ago when João had taken him along to visit a friend in Sao Paulo where he really had a chance to see what was going on in the 'real society' outside the heavily specialized atmosphere of a slave breeding, breaking, training, and sales facility that made up the essence of João's 'ranch.' João friend's estate was some 55 miles away from Sao Paulo - a secluded spot along the coast, much like João's ranch.

But, in transit, Christian saw slaves were now everywhere the eye could see in Brazil doing practically everything imaginable. They were easy to spot - almost always stripped to the buff or with most of their body showing; usually an overseer within a whip's length distance from them; and often manacled by their feet, their hands, or their neck. Some had been branded with their owner's mark, especially those owned by a business or corporation. All had a clearly visible slave identification mark tattooed where everyone could easily spot the number and a scanner could read the bar code.

The scenes he remembered in Brazil from three years ago were no different that those throughout America now other than the language being used to command the slaves in their tasks.

On that Sao Paulo trip, I remembered I noticed it didn't take long for almost all slaves to acquire a decent musculature - their hard work required it along with a tanned hide to protect them from the sun. Consequently, many slaves, especially the slaves in their late teens or twenties, were often nice to look at with their muscular builds, their nice physiques, and all of them totally exposed for public view. Many of them showed hard a good deal of the time. By that time, I understood this was due to most owners not allowing their slaves any sexual relief except as a rarely earned reward. (Christian chuckled to himself that he'd be hard all the time too if he couldn't get off regularly!). Thinking back, I reflected that even then I could figure out why slaves were rapidly finding their ways into their owner's beds. Again, Christian reflected, the Brazilian slaves were no different than America's slaves now.

Just recently, my friend Will here in New York had purchased a handsome and most muscular 18-year-old black boy as a gardener. It wasn't three days until that boy was being fucked by his new owner on a regular basis and had learned to give a great blow job within two weeks. By the third week of ownership, the black boy had been loaned to me overnight in exchange for loan of my own brown slave I had brought from Joáo on my trip down to his ranch. After one night with that boy, he reminded me of Niger, the black slave I had enjoyed so much on my visit to Joáo's ranch and I vowed I'd purchase a pure black within a month if I could find one looking anywhere near as good as this well hung (and I must say most compliant) black boy. As my friend Will pointed out, you bought a slave to do a job, like gardening. But that didn't mean their duties stopped there. He advised me to keep that in mind when I was buying any slave for some specific job to be done - there was always the possibility they could serve you sexually as well.

Sex or not, slaves were now being used for practically everything throughout all 50 states. There was practically nothing where slaves couldn't be effectively utilized within American society.

Again, I reflected on my memories of my visit to Joáo's friend, Colombo, over three years ago. When Joáo and I arrived at his friend's estate, Colombo had obviously embraced the easy availability of slaves nowadays. I noticed naked slaves seemed to be everywhere, but João, used to all this, barely looked at them. It was obvious Colombo had most anything available, especially livestock with two legs, that he could possibly want. As Colombo had graciously showed me around (kindly switching to English for my comfort), he said he had a dozen slaves altogether now and was thinking of buying a few more in that there was always something for them to do outside of just looking pretty and making themselves available at any time for his pleasure and amusement.

I had asked him at the time if he ever had trouble with any of his slaves.

"Never, never, Christian," he replied adamantly. "Buy from a good reputable dealer, like João here. They make sure they're completely trained before they sell them off. You buy a slave cheap from a shoddy dealer and you're likely to end up with a slave without a lick of training, a resentful attitude in his eyes, and a lot of trouble. You can spot a rogue slave easy enough, Christian. They generally have a lot of whip scars all over their body showing you they haven't responded to their training or, more likely, they haven't had any, a wild look of rebellion in their eyes, and they're generally kept in close restraints. A well trained slave doesn't need restraints, has a look of total acceptance in his eyes even when you're fondling him, and he seems like he's eager to find an owner. That's why it's important to handle a slave thoroughly before signing the ownership papers: a well trained slave is used to having his genitals manipulated right in public, has acclimated to being milked to test his output, and doesn't mind having his tits played with or his balls hefted and squeezed. That's important even if you're not buying a slave for sex purposes - accepting a good handling is a sure sign of accepting his status as nothing more than a piece of property - that's what they are now, after all!"

That advice seemed so familiar I wondered if every Brazilian school boy learned it by rote! I remembered at the time that João had given me almost exactly the same advice at some time or another.

Colombo had his chauffeur slave serving as a valet for our car upon our arrival, another dazzlingly beautiful slave to open the front door, an older slave butler to manage the house supervising a number of 18 to 20 year-old 'house slaves,' a most attractive bath slave to unpack my clothes and help me wash, a trio of stunning waiters that served dinner - one for each of us, a slew of rougher looking slaves keeping the grounds in order and managing the stables (he was into polo heavily), and he stated immediately that I was welcome to use any that appealed to me whenever I wanted. Colombo didn't need to turn a finger and could pick and choose among his slaves whenever he wanted sex of any type.

During that same venture, Colombo, João and I had visited a slave dealer that very afternoon in Sao Paulo in that Colombo was looking for yet another slave and João enjoyed studying the competition. Both thought the visit would be instructive for me since I was so 'naive' about slaves at that time. We visited the most prestigious and, according to João, certainly the priciest slave dealer in Sao Paulo.

The dealership was a long way from the seedy little stalls you saw slaves being sold at throughout the city of Sao Paulo. This one looked, well, sort of like a fine jeweler's sales room: lots of marble floors, glistening glass windows, crystal chandeliers, and the best quality leather furniture.

A salesman dressed impeccably greeted the three of us promptly.

"Did you have an appointment?" he politely asked.

"Yes, I'm Colombo Sanchez. I have a 5 o'clock appointment."

"Of course, Senor Sanchez. We're all set up to give your friends a little tour of our facility which will include an overview of our training facility, some of the current inventory in our holding pens, and, if you wish, we can arrange viewing of available stock in our sales room which will be stocked with drinks and snacks for your enjoyment. I might add, Senor Sanchez, your bank called as instructed and has given us clearance to charge any purchases you might want to make to your account. We'll handle all the paperwork, of course, as you have requested before when you bought stock from us, so a purchase is simply a gentleman's agreement if that's all right with you."

"Fine," Colombo replied.

"In that case, let's start with a quick view of our intake room - that's where we keep fresh stock just coming in that we've purchased. Totally untrained, totally unprepared for the market, just raw material that will take a lot of work and polish before it's marketable. But I thought your friends would be interested as well as yourself, possibly."

"I'm sure my friends would be interested and I'm always curious about new stock - it can always be trained to exact specification, after all," Columbo acknowledged the salesman.

With that, the salesman led the three of us into a large warehouse-type facility holding hundreds of individual cages and cells, most of which held an unwashed, naked body either clinging to the bars peering out in desperation, or sunk back in fatigue and despair. I did notice the bodies were basically show quality despite their dirt and grime and the smell was fairly well controlled by huge ventilation fans located throughout the building. The cages all had open mesh floors above a drain-like arrangement so that body waste could be flushed away every 15 minutes or so with an automatic flushing machine.

I was fascinated and could see from just a cursory inspection why the dealership had purchased them: they all showed a lot of promise once properly processed and trained. Most of them seemed to have a rough idea of what lay ahead for them. They'd been around long enough to have observed for themselves what slaves did and what the expectations were for slaves in today's society. Their worry and apprehension was as to how they could acclimate to the rigorous training they would be subjected to; what their new owners would be like; and just what they would be expected to do by those new owners. But they were smart enough to know that being purchased by a high priced dealer noted for handling quality goods was a good start at being a slave. They were likely to be well trained for their future life; were likely to sell to a well-heeled owner; and were likely to sell for a very high price. They weren't so dumb they didn't realize that the more paid for the goods; in general the better the goods would be treated.

"I was planning on showing your friends one of our training facilities. But, Senor Sanchez, I'm sure you're well familiar with the training routines we employ here. If you would like, I can have a slave take you back to the viewing rooms where you can begin looking over stock we're offering today."

"I'll stay with my friends. The tour won't take long and it's always instructive to see slaves in the midst of their training," Colombo responded in his gracious tone.

The next room the salesman showed us was one of the dealer's training facilities, in this case the salesman had chosen to visit the sex training facility. The salesman said all slaves sold by the dealership, regardless of what they were presumably purchased for, received full sexual training so they could satisfy the desires of almost any master or mistress that may purchase them.

"A slave never knows when an owner might take a fancy for his body. It's far better for a slave if he knows exactly what to expect and how to best handle the demands made upon him. Don't you agree?"

"Of course," Colombo promptly agreed. "Besides, he'll probably change hands several times at the minimum, so a slave never knows what his next owner might want regardless of who buys him the first time around."

"Exactly, Senor Sanchez," the salesman replied, obviously pleased his customer was interested in the training process. "Although most slaves in this price range can hardly expect to not be used by someone or other in their new home. It might be a master or mistress, one of their sons or daughters, a visiting friend or business colleague, a dinner guest, or perhaps their overseer or house steward. A slave never really knows who might find his body enjoyable."

It was obvious once we entered the room just how well trained the slaves from this particular dealership were going to be. During the brief visit, it was clear sucking, taking a good fucking, giving a good fuck, licking, rimming, and almost everything imaginable was being tutored. The slaves in training were intent on their tasks and barely noticed there were visitors in the room watching them. Either that, or part of their training had included learning to accept the fact others would be watching them in sexual activities in their new lives.

"All of these seem to accept their duties pretty well. Has it taken long to get them to this point?" I ventured to ask.

"A few weeks, generally. At first, we generally get some resistance. But once they discover sex of most any type - not just the type they're probably used to already - has pleasures of its own, the resistance just flows away. Sex training is mainly teaching the slave he can enjoy being used for sex - not as much as his user, probably - but still there's some pleasure in the acts themselves. Of course, they must learn their main function is to bring pleasure to whoever is using them - they're not in somebody's bed to pleasure themselves!" he chortled at the very thought of it.

"That would especially be true when they're forbidden to shoot off, I imagine, like when a mistress might want to use a stud over and over before she's totally satisfied," I ventured a comment again despite my lack of experience in this area.

"Exactly, sir," the salesman said. "A slave has to learn his enjoyment is within parameters set by his user - not himself. It's a hard lesson to learn, but it can be learned in a few weeks at most."

"And, if they don't?" João asked, never revealing his dealership was much larger and much more elaborate than this one.

"The whip is always instructive, sir," the salesman said with a smirk.

The sex training room had a heavy smell of sweat and cum permeating the room which gave it a heady atmosphere that was arousing in and of itself. I couldn't help but speculate on how long it would take to get me "fully trained" as the salesman put it and shared this thought with João, standing beside me.

"An hour or so from what I've seen back at my ranch," João whispered as we both tried to control our laughter.

"I don't want to hurry you, sirs, but I'd like to show Senor Sanchez some of the slaves we have on display for immediate sale - all fully trained and with a 90-day guarantee, of course."

"Yes, it will be interesting to see just what you've got available today," Colombo responded. "I take it there's a set price on the goods if they're not up for auction, like before?"

"Yes, we continue to have a suggested selling price listed for each one," the salesman said, patting a little book he had in his hand. "Of course, we offer 5% off for cash or credit card purchases and we offer a discount for multiple purchases on the same day. Perhaps your friends might be interested in a purchase as well, Senor Sanchez," he added hopefully. "Even if you're not in the market, you may see some goods you see some use for," he continued, his eyes sparkling as he was obviously referring to a body so appealing we couldn't do without buying it on the spot.

"Discounts? How much?" João asked with his usual professional demeanor.

"Ten percent off the total for two purchases; 15% for three purchases; 20% for four. After that, it's 25% up until 10 purchases; then it's 35% and even greater for large quantity purchases," the salesman responded by rote.

We entered the display room and I was impressed. Even João seemed to be impressed. First, there was a nice variety. Second, all the stock was obviously top quality. Third, even a cursory inspection revealed the stock had fully accepted the fact they were property there to be sold. I reminded myself any slave I bought in the future (outside of the handsome brown slave I had already bought from João) in New York would have to be at this level of quality or I'd eventually be disappointed with the slave. But, with further inspection and João's coaching, it was quickly apparent even this quality dealer had a large variety on sale: from the fresh to the well used; from the young to the past their prime; from the eager to those accepting but lacking that extra spark of enthusiasm. And the pricing, João pointed out to me, certainly revealed the dealership knew what the qualities were worth in the marketplace.

"Is this all you have available today?" Colombo asked rather pointedly.

"No, we can show you others. Any particular preferences?" the salesman answered.

"The best quality you've got," Colombo replied immediately. "Remember I'm a repeat customer who has dealt here for years."

With that subtle reminder of the buyer's expectations, the salesman took the three of us to another room, less elegantly furnished - obviously a storage area with an outside exercise yard.

"As you probably remember, Senor Sanchez, It you'd like, you can check out any of these boys in private. We have a small but comfortable room available for customers interested in trying a boy out for themselves before purchase. Just to make sure!" the salesman said pointing to a nicely decorated cottage about 50 feet away. "We understand that buying a slave from us is a major investment and customers often appreciate a trial run so to speak. That same privilege extends over to your friends, of course, Senor Sanchez."

"I thought you guaranteed your stock?" João countered.

"We do, sir. But still, a lot of customers prefer to thoroughly test out a slave before purchasing."

"Most dealers offer testing in public," João whispered to me. "My place certainly does in that many people are buying slaves for resale, not for their own use necessarily. Therefore, they see no need in private testing - neither they nor certainly not the slave being used have any privacy concerns. Some people I sell to are simply agents for potential owners who might not be interested and don't want to bother with the hassle of buying a slave themselves. And some of my customers have agents buy slaves merely as gifts they give out to their corporate clients or good friends in which case they just want to make sure the slave can perform sexually in public as well as in private."

The salesman noticed João whispering to me and interpreted it as a request to test the slaves out publicly.

"I understand, sir. Check them out all you want. Are there any out here or in the other room that you find of possible interest?"

"Yes," Colombo interjected. "I'll like to buy the half-breed displayed on a pole selling for $310,000; the black boy with the huge dick you're asking $430,000 for; the pure white American boy at $455,000; and the 18-year-old brown teenager selling for $298,000. That would give me four for a discount of 20% off the total with another 5% off for cash. That's 1.12 million roughly. I'll buy all four for 1.1 million even."

"You're quick with figures, Senor Sanchez," the salesman said, somewhat astonished.

"Yes, I'm not wealthy by accident," Colombo replied rather haughtily.

"Let me check with the owner of the dealership, sir. I don't want to pay that $20,000 additional discount out of my own pocket," he replied anxiously.

"Tell him that's only $5,000 off each slave and at the prices he's charging, that's nothing," Colombo replied.

"Well, there's always some negotiation," the salesman admitted and he scurried to see the owner of the establishment.

"Does your friend Colombo always decide things this fast?" I asked João, astonished myself. "I thought we came to buy just one slave."

"Colombo doesn't like to dilly-dally around and I suppose he liked the looks of those four. He's getting a good deal on them if the dealer acquiesces to his offer," Joáo replied.

"How about it, Joáo? Could you do any better on these four?" Colombo asked.

"No, my friend," Joáo replied with a big smile. "In fact, at that price, I may buy them off of you and take them back to my dealership for a quick, but profitable resale."

Within minutes, the salesman returned with an elderly gentleman Colombo instantly recognized from his country club.

"Well, Colombo, into buying some more meat, are you?" the man said laughingly. He glanced at the four selected for purchase. "Mighty pricey meat at that. Well, what the hell, as the price you're paying, $20,000 discount isn't too hard to swallow. They're yours at 1.1 mil and I don't think for a minute you'll regret paying that for them."

"Neither do I or I wouldn't be here buying," Colombo said.

Turning to Joáo, the owner acknowledged him as a fellow dealer. "Senor de Silva, it's an honor to have you visit this small establishment. What do you think, although I'm surprised my good friend Colombo didn't buy his new meat from you. Are you planning to resell this stock at your own dealership in the near future?"

"Well, I just might when our mutual friend here has his fill of them. And, in answer to your first question, I heartily approve of your dealership. Nice presentation, nice selection, obviously good training. And your salesman was properly zealous in trying to dispose of some of your properties for you," Joáo glanced at the salesman who blushed at the high compliment. "Feel free to visit my own modest establishment whenever you get a chance. It's always interesting to compare our operations."

"I may just do that, but if I buy any stock there, I expect the same discount I'm giving you on these pieces of meat," the dealer laughed as he slapped Joáo on the back heartily.

"You buy four high priced ones off of me and I'll give you a lousy $20,000 off list," Joáo countered.

"The salesman said you didn't even try them out before buying them," the dealer said bemused turning to Colombo. "Are you that straight or fucking slaves isn't your thing?"

"I enjoy a slave now and then as well as the best of them, but I've got plenty of time for that later. I thought a guarantee was a guarantee. If I don't think they perform up to standards, I fully intend to bring them right back! I just wasn't in the mood right now in the heat of the afternoon."

"Fair enough," the dealer said, handing Colombo all the ownership papers already signed and notarized and now delivered by his secretary. "You want me to ship them to your estate or are you going to take them with you. If so, it will be these boys first ride in a Maserati Quattro, I'll wager," letting Colombo know the dealer was even aware of what type of car the three of them had arrived in.

"I'll take them with me if they're really clean."

"They are. We always polish them inside and out before displaying them."

"Good. Three in the trunk, and that $480,000 black in the front seat with me. I don't want him bruised in any way at that price and, besides, I want to see if that prick's as big and yummy as it looks."

"It is, Senor Sanchez" the dealer assured him. "And enjoy!"

João told me later that Colombo did enjoy his new purchases over and over during the next few days. He added that Colombo decided they were well worth what he had paid for them, especially when he knew he could get a lot more from them peddled to the right people, including João's own dealership. In the interim, he fully intended to take full advantage of his investment. It was obvious right from the beginning the training was so good there would be no question of returning them under the guarantee.

CHAPTER 9

I now had two slaves under my roof. The magnificent brown sex slave João had sold me in Brazil over three years had arrived about a week or so after I got back to New York City from that trip and has been in my bed ever since. And, just a month or so ago, my friend Will sold me his 18-year-old black gardener I enjoyed so much when he loaned him to me a while back, having bought a new, even fresher red haired boy to take over the gardening duties at his suburban home.

[It seems Will had attended an obscure uncle's funeral in Kansas and saw the boy for sale at a local dealership. A court mandated sale, the boy had only been 16 when he was first arrested for car theft, judged guilty, and sentenced to slavery when he reached 18. The court then had the boy sent to the regional state slave training facility and there the boy learned what his new life held for him. Fortunately, he was well built, well hung, and very good looking and took to his training well. Sent back to the court when his training was completed, he was assigned to a local dealer who sold him to Will just two days after they had him in their pens.

Once purchased and in Will's New York home, the young slave did all of the gardening as well as serving Will's sexual needs.]

I made sure both of my slaves kept themselves in top shape, having them practice their training routines daily when not in use. Both slaves knew I would get rid of them instantly if they ever lost any of their abilities to please me or any of my guests.

Having two slaves at my disposal was a nice arrangement. I could choose brown or black dependent on my mood and have both if I was feeling particularly horny. When I wasn't up to fucking them, they fucked each other for my amusement. Similarly, they performed at small dinner parties for the amusement of my guests, usually such tableaus ending with them being loaned out to first one guest and then another until all my guests were satiated with compliant slave flesh. I could also loan one of the slaves out to a business associate overnight as a special favor without emptying my own bed in the process. The slave chow to feed them was cheap enough and both were easy enough to keep caged in the basement of my townhouse when I wasn't around. After I had bought the young black, I wondered how I had managed with just one slave - the handsome brown I had bought in Brazil. Of course, I mused, not long after the brown slave had arrived from Brazil, I couldn't imagine how I had managed with no slave at all before his arrival. Slaves seemed to have an addictive quality to them!

I wasn't long after I had added Will's black slave to my 'staff' that João called to tell me he would be taking a business trip to New York the following week and wondered if I could put him up.

"Put you up, João?" I laughed. "You make it sound like you're asking me to set a pup tent up on the roof. Of course, I'll 'put you up,' as you call it. In fact, I may even be damn decent and actually host you, you old rascal. You know damn well I've got a guest suite in the townhouse just waiting for you, I've got full time to devote to your visit, and," I paused, "I've even got a beautiful brown slave you sold me you've fucked many a time before and who will be more than happy to have you fuck him again. In fact, João," I paused dramatically, "I've even got a new 18-year-old American black slave I've named 'Beauty' that, to the best of my knowledge, has never been fucked by a Brazilian master. I'm sure he'll look forward to it."

"Well, I didn't want to put you out or anything," João laughed, "although the accommodations sound interesting and I'm not talking about that damn guest suite of yours. Maybe I won't need to bring a slave or two along with me as I had originally planned."

"That depends on what you were bringing, João. As you probably remember, I've never been adverse to a little variety now and then and I've got plenty of spare cages in the basement."

"Well, I was thinking of giving Thor a short break from studding, Christian, and he's never lost that rather charming resentment of being fucked himself. I know you appreciated that in him as much as I do. Fucking a slave who doesn't mind it too much is one thing - fucking a slave who hates every minute of it is a much more interesting experience, don't you agree?"

I laughed as I remembered when I first asked Thor whether he liked being fucked and, without hesitation, he answered with a simple "no." It did make fucking him more fun somehow.

"I do agree now that you bring it up, João. And, you know, João, I haven't bedded down a blond since I fucked Thor. Can you believe it?"

"Thor is in, then, Christian. Anything else that would turn you on?" João chuckled.

"Thor's plenty as a house gift, João, but if you bring something else, surprise me," I replied. "When can I expect you? We can pick you up at Kennedy in the Bentley - yes, I still have the same one that matches the brown slave's hide color that you sold me."

"I'm coming in my private jet, Christian. Just got it last week and want to try it out. We'll land at a private airport in New Jersey, just across the river from you, and save you a long trip. Therefore, I can get there anytime you want, but it will take me a good seven hours air time to get there, so how about 3 P.M. next Wednesday afternoon your time? We'll land at the Rogers Air Service airport, right off of Interstate 1, Exit 15, first exit after you leave Lincoln Tunnel. It should take you about a half hour to get there from your town house with mid-afternoon traffic. Think that brown boy I sold you can manage chauffeuring that Bentley there without too much trouble?"

"I'll be there to pick you up, João, and yes, 'Rico' as I named that brown slave, can manage driving me there. But if you're coming by private jet, I'm sure you're going to have more than Thor along with you. I can't imagine you on a seven-hour trip in a private jet just sitting there reading a magazine and fucking Thor can't possibly take seven hours, resentful or not. My guess is you'll have one or two more slaves onboard just for your own amusement and then you'll claim it was simply so I could enjoy them. I know you like a book by now, Joáo," I joked. "But, just remember, I've got 'Rico' for you to reacquaint yourself with as well as a beautiful piece of black fresh just coming into full manhood. If you bring Thor, that ought to be enough for the two of us."

"Maybe for you, Christian," Joáo laughed. "But you forget I'm used to having hundreds of slaves around at any given time. You don't want me to feel starved, do you?"

"Oh, for Christ's sake, Joáo. Bring whatever you want. As I said, there's plenty of cages in my basement and I'm always open to some new slave meat."

"I knew you'd see it my way, Christian. See you next Wednesday and lay in plenty of slave chow and K-Y," Joáo chuckled as he hung up.

I wondered just what sort of business Joáo needed to conduct in New York. It was either management of his holdings, like when I had first met him, or something to do with buying or selling slaves. It could be he would have the new private jet stuffed full of slaves he was delivering to a New York buyer, including the heavily used stud, Thor.

I reflected on the blond stud, Thor, briefly. Even when I was in Brazil three years ago, he had already fucked more at age 21 than most men do in three lifetimes. By now, he surely was near the wearing out point. Joáo used to brag that he had sired 1000 new properties to sell - by now, Lord knows how many wenches he had knocked up? !500? 2000? Four times a day, seven days a week - the only relief the white stud got was when he was being fucked himself by Joáo or one of the ranch's guests. I wondered if Thor, by this time, actually welcomed being fucked by whomever just to break the monotony and to give his balls some relief. I didn't think for a minute, though, that Thor was on that plane just for my benefit. Joáo always enjoyed fucking him, simply because he believed the slave resented it so, and I couldn't help wondering if Thor had been sold to someone here in New York and wouldn't find out until his new master or mistress appeared to pick him up. He was, after all, surely nearing the end of his stud run and João was always one to sell off before a slave depreciated too much.

———————

João's private jet was larger than I thought it would be. I envisioned the model holding 5 or 6 people; this model looked like it could handle 10 or more - considerably more if most of the seats had been removed and replaced by small slave cages stacked one on top of another which I suspected was the case.

When João stepped off the plane, everything went smoothly. He had electronically handled the paperwork for his entry and even set up the forms on his computer to pay the import fees on any slaves he sold here in the United States. When Rico recognized his former master, he dropped to his knees and bowed his head as João acknowledged his old slave with a ruffle through the slave's hair.

"Master," Rico said in greeting reverently.

"You still look good enough to fuck," João acknowledged the greeting. "Your owner has invited me to do just that when I get settled in," João laughed, "and I have little doubt that I will - just to see if you are as good in bed as you used to be back in Brazil. Or has the big city dampened your ardor a bit?"

"No, master, this slave is as good as he's ever been," Rico replied humbly. "You'll see when you fuck me, master."

"Glad to hear it, slave," João said as he went over to kiss me on both cheeks - a custom he still retained.

"Welcome to the Big Apple, João," I said, "it's been way too long!" After all these years, I felt myself quickly responding to him, namely a huge hard-on which João noticed instantly.

"You ARE glad to see me, Christian," he chuckled, eyeing my crotch meaningfully. "I'd be all hard and leaking too if I hadn't of overdone it on the plane a bit with some of the stock I brought along, but the sentiment is there just the same," as he gave me a really big hug, squeezing my butt as he did so.

"I just knew you've have more than Thor on that plane," I said as five stunning slave specimens stretched and yawned as they crawled out of their cages and came down the steps one by one.

Each was very muscular, totally naked, body shaved, and ringed around the neck, around their balls, and through their tits. All five were hugely endowed and had exceptionally handsome faces. Each was a different color: Nordic blonde, Mediterranean dark olive, Nigerian jet black, Polynesian brown, and Chinese yellow. All were fully developed but none looked to be over 23 or so. When they reached the tarmac, each went into full display position with their heads lowered, obviously expecting me to look them over.

As I took the five in, standing with their legs spread wide apart and their hands grasping the back of their slave collars with their banded genitals thrust out for my convenience in handling them, another handsome slave was coming down the steps. It was Thor - handsome as ever and seemingly none the worse for wear. His huge prick and balls were just as big as I remembered and his rampant erection indicated he still had no trouble in displaying his assets properly.

"You brought six slaves, Joáo?" I chortled. "With my two, that's eight slaves between the two of us. What are you trying to do, kill me?"

"Nonsense, Christian. I want you to try each of these boys out when you get a chance, but, actually, all six are potentially sold. That's why I had to come to New York - a buyer has an option on these six he picked off the internet inventory, but wanted to personally inspect them, of course, before plunking down hard cash. I've got a 10% non-refundable deposit on each of them to guarantee I wouldn't loose the cost of bringing them up here if he decides not to exercise his option. But, what the hell, even if he doesn't - it will be easy enough to find a buyer here in New York. The market's hot here right now and prices are astronomical. A good time to sell off excess stock - you might think of it yourself, Christian."

I strolled over to the six on full display (Thor had now joined the line and he too was properly displaying himself) and gave each a rather cursory inspection, mainly weighing their balls in my hand, running my hand over their sculptured pecs, tweaking their nipple rings, and fondling their long, thick dicks to a full throbbing erection. All stood perfectly still for the body inspection with their pelvises thrust forward for my convenience.

"They probably think you're the one buying them," João laughed. "But God knows how many times they're going to be looked over before they're someone else's property."

"They are damn tempting, João," I commented. "You shouldn't have any trouble selling them. Hell, I'm tempted myself."

"Don't decide anything until you fuck them, Christian. Then you'll know they not only look pretty but are perfectly trained to bring the upmost pleasure to any new owner," João boasted.

The blond, the dark olive, and the jet-black slave all blushed deeply and had tears running down their cheeks as the wanton use of their bodies was discussed so openly with this total stranger. João noticed it also.

"Slaves showing a little shame and humiliation makes them all the more attractive, don't you think, Christian? I know it generally adds a good 5% to their price when they're auctioned off. Those three getting all teary on you are fairly new to their slavery and just fresh out of training. The Polynesian boy was born into it and the Chinese boy had at least three masters before I bought him. And, of course, Thor has been around forever - he's well past the crying and blushing stage, but," João laughed, "he still resents the hell out of getting fucked up his ass."

"Frankly, João, I'm old fashioned enough to think I would blush too when I was standing in front of a total stranger with someone's hand around my prick and all the talk is about fucking me when it's convenient."

"That's the Catholic in you, Christian. All three of those embarrassed boys you're playing around with were heavy in religion in their previous lives. They still don't seem to understand nothing is a 'sin' when you're a slave and you're ordered to do something you were taught was wrong when you were free. What's 'right' and what's 'wrong' isn't in a slave's province - those things are up to his master or mistress. You watch, a few months from now and all that blushing and shame and looks of humiliation and crying will all be gone. Too bad. That sort of thing jacks their price up, as I said."

By then, a small slave delivery van had arrived that João had arranged for transport of his stock and all six were ordered to crawl into the van's small cages. Christian had seen the special Acme

Moving "Livestock Delivery" trucks all over New York but never knew what the insides were like until now.

"Are you sure you can cage all six in your basement, Christian?" João asked. "I can have them put in a public kennel if you prefer. There are a number of them not far from your townhouse that do a decent job of taking care of stock in transit."

"No problem, João. I've got plenty of spare cages and I stocked up on lots of slave chow. Rico can take care of feeding and watering them and can even get them all cleansed out and polished when that potential buyer wants to look them over. Besides," I smiled, "it's sort of inconvenient to go to the public kennel and check them out every time we want to fuck them. We'd spend as much time going back and forth to the kennel than we would screwing them."

"Point well taken," João said as he gave the delivery van driver my address and told him to take his time so he wouldn't beat us back.

"No problem," the delivery van driver said cheerfully. "I've got two more pickups here in Jersey before I head back to Manhattan."

"You got enough cage space?" João asked the driver.

"No problem," the driver said cheerfully as he thumbed through his papers. "Let's see here. Pickup of three females and one male being transferred from the 'Paradise, Inc.' branch not far from here to the branch in lower Manhattan - that's one of those huge brothel chains all over the East Coast. They always seem to be switching their stock from one location to another - I suppose it gives the customers at each location a constant supply of fresh ones to choose from. And five draft slaves just shipped in at the Newark airport from the Congo for delivery to the New York sanitation department. That's just nine more altogether and the truck's fitted with 20 cages, mister."

João signed some papers and got a receipt for his stock. Rico, always sexually excited when around new slaves, was fully erect as he opened the back door of the Bentley for us. Soon we were on our way to Manhattan.

"You're right, Christian," João observed enthusiastically, "Rico's hide is a perfect match for the car's upholstery. I can see why you keep the car."

"And Rico," I laughed. "As long as he doesn't fade on me. But I do make it a point to keep him out of the sun as much as I can. He'd be too dark otherwise."

"It's been three years since I've been up your ass, Rico," João said pointedly to the chauffeur. "You still put out as well as you did back in Brazil?"

"Yes, master," Rico responded with a big smile. "Even better, master."

"Well, we'll see about that before I leave, if that's alright with your master," João shot back.

"Yes, master," Rico said, glancing at me in the rear-view mirror to ascertain my wishes in the matter.

"Anytime you want, João. You're our guest here, remember, and everything, including both my slaves, are at your full disposal."

"Yes, master," Rico replied in response to my announcement and smiled invitingly at João in the mirror.

After we got back to my house, João took a long shower, fucked Rico, and took another shower before joining me for a late supper. The black boy I had named Beauty served the meal. He too had just body shaved, cleaned his insides out, showered, greased himself up, and oiled his body until it glistened in preparation for serving the meal. As usual, his dress was his polished collar, his tit rings, and his thick genital band. He managed to serve the entire meal, start to finish, with a full erection.

"The boy's well trained," João said, "and the food's delicious. Did the boy prepare it too?"

"Yes, he's quite a little cook, among other things," I said, happy the slave pleased my guest. "You want him in your bed tonight? He's unusually skilled for a slave so young."

"Why not?" João said. "But not before midnight or so. It'll take me that long to juice up again reacquainting myself with Rico just a short time ago. And, Christian, I'll probably be sleeping in tomorrow morning, but Beauty here can slip out after I'm asleep to make sure your breakfast is served when you want it. Tomorrow night, I'd like to get in the saddle with Rico again, if the invitation still holds."

"Sure does, whenever you want," I replied, toying with my dessert by now, a delicious custard Beauty had prepared to perfection.

"Which of my boys did you want to start with?" Joáo said. "Thor first?"

"Later," I said. "Tonight I'd like to sample that new blonde and that Mediterranean slave as a starter. It's been a while since I've had any white slaves. Thor can wait to get fucked a little while longer. I really got turned on when those slaves teared up when I was handling them. You're right, Joáo. It does add something to their appeal. Will they turn bright red in embarrassment and start sobbing when I fuck them?"

"Probably, but they'll be totally cooperative nevertheless. They've been thoroughly trained to deliver total satisfaction no matter what you want them to do. The blushing and crying is just a bonus. But, you're smart to fuck them tonight. If everything goes well, someone else will be fucking their new property by tomorrow night. You sure you don't want the other three new ones while you have a chance? I can't guarantee what will be in those cages by tomorrow night, Christian."

"Two's plenty, but if I wake up in the morning really all charged up, I'll have Rico bring me up some others when he returns the two. Seems a shame not to sample all the goodies when they're as close as a basement cage, Joáo."

The next morning, Beauty served a nice breakfast, although it was obvious he hadn't gotten a full night's sleep and he was walking sort of bull-legged like his butt was mighty sore.

"Looks like you earned your keep last night, Beauty," I joked as I started in on my omelette.

"Yes, master. Your friend knows how to thoroughly use a slaveboy," Beauty replied in a non-judgmental tone.

"I've seem him fuck a slave, Beauty. He's pure master when it comes to fucking a slave - a little rough for the slave, maybe."

"Yes, master," Beauty smiled as he rubbed his ass knowingly.

Rico reported in by kneeling beside the breakfast table.

"Does Master need me for anything?" Rico asked.

"Everything all right down in the cages? Did you get all of them cleaned up inside and out, body shaved, oiled, greased, and fed and watered this morning, Rico?"

"Yes, master. I finished all that before I reported to you up here, master."

Rico looked at me, obviously seeking permission to add something to his report.

"Permission to speak, Rico," I said.

"Those are mighty handsome slaves down there. They should sell for a lot of money."

"Yes, Rico. Maybe," I snickered, "as much as I had to pay for your brown hide."

"Yes, master," Rico said, obviously proud he had brought a good price at his sale.

That afternoon, Joáo awoke, put on a few clothes and flew into action on his cell phone. Within an hour, a well-dressed man in his mid-thirties arrived at the town house and Joáo was showing him all six of his slaves, now gleaming in a fresh coat of body oil and in full display position in my living room. Rico and Beauty were behind me ready to help out in any way if they were needed. Both my slaves were quite excited at seeing some beautiful specimens of manhood being sold right in their master's living room.

Joáo's client was thorough, never hurried himself, and obviously knew exactly how to assess slave flesh. Each slave had every muscle and organ in his body prodded and pulled, pinched, and squeezed. His eyes, teeth, balls, tits, and prick received special inspection along with a slow, thorough examination of each slave's anal chute and throat with probing fingers, dildos and plugs, the last two of which he had brought with him in all sizes and shapes in a small suitcase. It took him a good hour to complete his examination which included every square inch of the slave's skin, his feet, his hair, and even his tongue and the insides of his nose and ears. If those slaves didn't feel like a piece of property before, they sure as hell did now, I thought to myself as I admired the client's complete and thorough assessment. Joáo's slaves stood up well to the exam despite an occasional gasp or moan as yet another aspect of their body was explored. The three that had blushed yesterday stood silently as tears spilled down their cheeks the entire time of the inspection, but, to their credit, they never flinched or resisted in any way to the probing fingers that treated them as nothing more than a piece of prime meat. Which, I thought to myself, is exactly what they are!

"Prime meat here, Joáo," the client announced at last. "I can't find a thing wrong with them, although, of course, what they'll be like in action is something else again. But, life's a gamble, isn't it. I'll take all of them at the option price."

"Even the stud slave?" Joáo asked, obviously pleased the sale had gone so smoothly.

"Even him, Joáo. As you said on the phone when we were discussing all this, he's probably nearing the end of his career in the rutting sheds, but there's a few hundred more slave pups probably left to be extracted from those big balls of his, and even if he dries up before that, he's still sellable as a decent bed buck. My wife's been asking for a new boy - this one should do just fine - lots of experience, excellent equipment, and still a handsome boy to look at. She'll be happy with him - I'll give the slave to her as an anniversary gift. That's the sort of present she likes - something she can actually use. And she'll like a boy that's spent years down in the rutting sheds - that will add a lot of excitement to him as far as she's concerned. Women! Who knows what goes through their minds? The stud she's got now is a black brute that's ugly as sin if you ask me - oh, he's hung like a horse - but he's just downright ugly. I never knew what she saw in him, but that's what she wanted at the time. Now she's grown tired of the black ape. I'm not surprised. This blond is as least clean looking and decent to look at, although he too is hung like a horse."

I looked at Thor as his future was being discussed. As usual, his face revealed little, but he didn't look displeased. I supposed, like most stud slaves put into retirement, he expected as much. Most former studs were sold off as bed bucks to mistresses and masters who valued experience and rigid training.

"I promised my friend he could fuck the blond stud before I sold him off," Joáo said. "He last fucked him when he was visiting me in Brazil and took a fancy to the boy's talents. He asked me yesterday if he could fuck him again and I promised him he could."

"That's exactly why I am buying him - well, that and for my wife's use as I mentioned. Something about fucking a stud slave that's sort of exciting. But we can work this out, Joáo. I'll fuck him just as soon as we get the paperwork done if your friend doesn't mind loaning me a place to do it and then your host can fuck him all he wants overnight. My steward can't pick the new purchases up until tomorrow afternoon anyway."

With that, the six slaves changed hands and Rico returned all but Thor back to their cages in the basement. Thor was then taken to the spare bedroom to await usage by Joáo's client. Joáo signed all the sales papers which he had already prepared on his laptop back in Brazil, notified the customs office of the sales price and gave them permission to charge the import fee to his account, and logged in the slaves' GPS codes to the national slave registry along with their new owner's name and address. His client, meanwhile, arranged transfer of the necessary funds to cover the purchase to Joáo's account. Within 15 minutes, the paperwork was completed and Joáo could see the proper amount had been transferred. Almost three-quarters of a million dollars had changed hands with that one transaction, but, after all, the goods were certainly premium. Joáo told Rico to take his client to where Thor was waiting and within 45 minutes the client was back, fastening his belt.

"That was fast," Joáo chuckled. "The slave was satisfactory, I assume?"

"No problem fucking the slave, Joáo. It's just that I have another business appointment within the hour. As much as I wanted to, I just didn't have the time right now to fuck the slave thoroughly as I would have preferred. But I've got plenty of time when he's stabled in my own house and he was more than satisfactory for an afternoon quickie. But, Joáo, you'll need to have him flushed out completely before your host beds him down."

"Stuffed him full of cum, my friend?" Joáo chuckled.

"Afraid so, Joáo."

With that, the client left and I never saw him again. As he said, his agent picked up the six new purchases the next afternoon rather late and that was the last I ever saw of any of them. By then, though, I had had a chance to sample all of them, starting with Thor an hour after the client had left and as soon as he had been flushed out, given a shower, and relubed.

When Thor was delivered to my room, I saved my questions until after I had pumped a full load into him, noting his resentment at being fucked by another male was as evident as ever. It seemed to me that after all this time, he would have gotten over it, although the quality of the fuck he offered up was right up there with the best.

He was flat on his back with his legs over my shoulders and I was still well inside him when I started my questioning as I stared into his eyes.

"What do you think of your new owner?" I asked.

"O.K. Master," was the non-committal answer.

"No, Thor, I what to know what you think of being sold off. You won't be making slave babies anymore it seems and you'll get to fuck for a mistress' enjoyment, it seems. Well, that, and taking your new master up your butt too, apparently."

Thor grunted as I drove my prick deeper into him and began slowly pumping him once again.

"A slave doesn't decide what's going to happen in his life, master," Thor said. "But, since you asked me, master, I'll tell you. Sounds like my new life will be a lot better than I hoped. I won't be under the whips in an emerald mine yet; I won't be humping worn-out old breeding wenches four or five times a day down in a stinking rutting shed, and, if the master's wife is about his same age, I won't have to fuck an ancient dried up mistress yet. Sounds like all I'll be doing is fucking the mistress whenever she wants anyway she wants it; taking a fucking whenever the master wants it; and, of course, probably entertaining both my new master's and mistress' friends when they want. But Master João told me I'll still be studding now and then for slave production. He said the new master bought me to lease out when he finds an opportunity, but they would be short-term leases like renting me out to small slaveholders to impregnate all their women slaves on one short visit and then rent me out to another for a week or two - that sort of thing. He told me the new master planned to keep my balls drained - just not as much as I was used to and sort of off and on."

"You're still going to be taking it up the ass, like now, Thor," I pointed out as I thrust into him even deeper.

"Yes, master, but it still sounds better than before," Thor insisted, the resentment at being fucked clearly evident in his eyes even as he pronounced he was going to a better life. "For a slave, I'm pretty lucky compared to what we heard from others in that

Acme Moving delivery trunk yesterday. All we slaves sold by Master Joáo yesterday are, compared to those others," Thor added. "Of course, we'll all real good-looking and hung heavy - that sure helps if you're a slave."

"I thought there were just some brothel and draft slaves in that truck, Thor?" I asked.

"Yes, master, that's right. Those brothel slaves were good looking like us, master, but whereas we get fucked now and then by a master, they get fucked around the clock year after year and, they said, by those so down and out they can't even afford a slave for themselves. So they have to service the old, the sick, the disabled, the smelly poor people, - people no one else who has a choice will fuck. That male whore among them could barely get it up anymore, he told me, and his ass was so stretched he couldn't get it closed anymore, no matter how hard he tried. And, master, those draft slaves were from somewhere in Africa I've never heard of and had only been rounded up by slave catchers a week or so ago. They'd been stripped of whatever clothes they had, branded, collared, and shackled; whipped good, and put on a plane for America. That's all they knew apparently, although I couldn't understand much of the strange language they spoke. But I could tell they didn't know shit about what was going to happen to them although they did seem to know about slaves - I did get out of them they had plenty of them back wherever they came from and they knew they were slaves now. The collars on their necks and the brands on their butts had told them that. Master, at least I always understand what's going on, even if I don't have any control over it."

It was easy to understand Thor's optimism about his new life and I had always appreciated his ability to put things in perspective. With that, both of us shut up and I concentrated on achieving the best orgasm I'd ever had with Thor - sort of a finale to my great experiences fucking him.

By the time the agent arrived to pick the six slaves up, I had fucked every single one of them. After Thor, I then had the two slaves who had been owned by others before Joáo bought them: the Chinese and the Polynesian boys. They were obviously very experienced in pleasuring a master. The handsome Chinese boy had exceptional sucking skills, while the Polynesian demonstrated complete mastery of his ass muscles after you were well up into him that sent you over the edge coupled with big juicy tits that were remarkably sensuous to suck. The black boy from Nigeria was the opposite of Thor. He delighted in being used by a male and there wasn't an ounce of resentment in him, no matter how much you rammed down his throat or up his butt. Either his training was remarkable or he was naturally gay - I suspected both - but it didn't matter. His new owner couldn't help but be pleased if providing sexual pleasure was any criteria! I wondered, however, how he would do with a mistress - but good slave training usually eliminates any potential problems like that.

João, of course, had already used all six of them heavily, both back in Brazil and, most recently, on the plane from Brazil, and, at least with two-thirds of them, here in my house. He told me he was certain their new owner would be pleased with them and was getting a good buy, even at the prices he got for them.

"What did he buy them for, João, other than Thor for his wife and himself?" I asked.

"Business gifts, Christian. He's into oil heavily, and deals a lot with most of the large oil companies owned by governments in the Middle East. It won't be long until those new purchases of his will find themselves in palaces in Dharan, Kuwait City, Abu Dhabi, Aden, and Tripoli among others. I've sold hundreds just like them for the same purpose. My client will give them at some point to a good customer as a guarantee the next big contract comes his way. After that, they'll be watering the lawns, driving the cars, cleaning the palaces, serving the meals, and all the other things slaves do these days for the super wealthy. But, in view of their looks, these boys will also spend a good deal of their time in their new owner's bedrooms. Those oil potentates are accustomed to such courtesies and, after all, their families have generally had slaves around for just that purpose for centuries now. It's just that now they can enjoy slaves from all over the world in all different colors with no difficulty at all. And, for the most part, those slaves never cost them a penny!"

"It's sort of weird to think of being given to someone as a 'gift,' don't you think, João?"

"No, it's just property like anything else - a bottle of booze, a new car, a nice new outfit to wear - what's the difference?"

"Well, if I were a slave, it would be the final degradation - just being given away as a gift to someone."

"Christian, you're so sentimental sometimes I wonder how you survive in this world," Joáo said rather disgusted. "But," he brightened, "maybe that's the charm in you I find so attractive. An incredible naivete about slaves. That, and," he reached over and squeezed my ass, "the fact you're still one of the best fucks I've ever had out of a free boy."

With that, Joáo and I renewed our acquaintance with each other's bodies and I discovered I found Joáo just as interesting as I ever had. Rico and Beauty would be put on hold until Joáo left and, of course, Joáo now had nobody but me to relieve him.

CHAPTER 10

Thinking I could put Rico and Beauty "on hold" during João's visit was ridiculous of course. João was completely attuned to having hundreds of slaves available to him at any time and trying to limit him just to my bed was absurd.

The next night, João and I reached new levels of enjoying each other's bodies. But, by 2 A.M. João asked if my two slaves could "at least" put on a little show for us as we were playing around and shortly after that, Rico and Beauty were staging one of their tableaus they often presented for my guests.

But, even before they dutifully started to fuck each other for our amusement, João started directing them, first having Beauty lower himself onto Rico's prick and then proceed to pump himself; next having Rico on all fours while Beauty fucked him. Neither slave was allowed to shoot off during their performances, especially difficult when João ordered the two slaves to suck each other off in a 69 position we could both view easily. Both slaves were covered in sweat with every muscle tensed as they performed, biting their lips as they struggled to keep from having the forbidden orgasm.

"Jesus, Joáo," I said as I watched the slaves performing while Joáo was languidly fucking me, "at least let them get some relief."

"Nonsense, Christian. It's good for slaves to practice self-control. Reminds them of what they are," was Joáo's reply as he pumped into me somewhat more vigorously.

Well, Joáo got his relief, deep within my rectum. And I got mine, deep down his throat a little later. But my poor slaves never did, at least when performing for us on top of a large library table in my bedroom where we could view them easily.

But relief did come for them the next morning. Joáo, waking up long before me, had supervised the preparation of a breakfast to his liking and Beauty, being a young black buck, had been milked to supply the fresh cum Joáo liked in his omelette as well as coating his breakfast rolls. But Joáo was ravenous and one omelette wasn't enough. Beauty's second milking yielded little and so Joáo had to make do with Rico's cum, certainly plenteous after all the stimulation he had the night before, but "not as sweet as a pure black's" according to Joáo's assessment.

By the time I arrived in the dining room, both Rico and Beauty were strangely flaccid and both looked a little sheep-faced as they brought me what I wanted: corn flakes and orange juice.

"Why aren't you hard?" I asked.

"Master, we've been.... we've been.. milked," Rico stammered out, his rich brown skin turning a strange shade of pink as he blushed in embarrassment.

"Milked dry, Master," Beauty added with a shamed look on his face. "Master Joáo milked us for his breakfast, Master."

"Omelettes and frosting for his breakfast roll?" I smirked.

"Yes, Master," the two slaves answered in unison, both amazed I could read their minds.

"Master Joáo is accustomed to that for breakfast. Back on his ranch, that's what he has every morning as far as I know," I informed them. "When I was there, he kept a nice-looking black slave with very large balls, still in his teens, in the kitchen just for that purpose."

I noticed Beauty shuttered at the revelation, realizing his probable fate if he belonged to Master Joáo.

"What's the problem, Christian?" Joáo burst into the room, freshly showered and dressed for the day by now. "Didn't Beauty realize slaves can be milked like any other animal" he laughed.

"He probably never thought about it, Joáo," I replied. "He's only belonged to my friend Will and I so far and doesn't know much about all the uses slaves are put to these days."

"Well, his innocence is appealing. I noticed when I fucked him, he was cooperative enough but responded like I was being a little rough. I'd like to see his reaction if he were in my training center back at the ranch. Those trainers of mine aren't noted for their gentleness," Joáo laughed, "and that's good because a slave never knows who or what he's going to be sold to. Some owners, I understand, really enjoy treating their slaves rough - very rough. I've even had a few buyers looking to replace stock they got too zealous with in their lovemaking and destroyed their own property in the process. Pretty stupid - destroying your own property but it's their money," Joáo sighed.

"Makes you wonder what happens to slaves given away as corporate gifts," I commented, thinking of the beautiful slaves Joáo sold yesterday right here in my living room. "Do you ever hear what happens to slaves just given away, Joáo?"

"Only from that client I sold to yesterday," Joáo said. "By the way, any of those frosted rolls left, Beauty?"

Beauty quickly exited to the kitchen and returned with a plate containing two more rolls, both glistening with his own creamy white cum. It was quite obvious he didn't like looking at how his manly output was being utilized that morning, but he properly knelt before Master Joáo for presentation of the rolls, his eyes downward in respect.

As Joáo took a bite into the roll, he slurped up the icing with his tongue and savored the treat before continuing to answer my question.

"My client doesn't get too much direct feedback but he does run into his gifts now and then when visiting his business associates. He claims since he only gives away the best looking, heaviest hung slaves he can buy, most of them end up as his associates' sex slaves where they get pampered and spoiled over time. He said one of his associates died once and the gift he had given him was returned but that slave was so cocky and full of himself by then he had to send him off for serious retraining before he could give him away again. The retraining center was harsh but thorough, and when the slave came back to him - at considerable expense for his new training, he added - he was fine to give away again. But, Christian, he added he thought the retraining center had sort of overdone it - the slave tremored and shook a lot when on display and was so eager to fulfill any command at all he came off as a beaten dog that never got over it if you know what I mean. My client said if he ran into a slave like that again - too big for their own britches - he'd just sell him on the open market for whatever he could get and suffer the losses. That, or just sell him off for his body parts."

"And what would you do under those circumstances, Joáo," I asked out of genuine curiosity, while I enjoyed the alarmed look in both Rico's and Beauty's eyes, now in slave display again.

"Well, it would depend, Christian," Joáo replied as he picked up the second roll and began licking off the 'frosting.' "First off, I'd see where the boy was originally trained or whether he was bred. If he'd been at a good training center, like the one I run, I'd just write him off as a loss and sell him for rendering. If a slave's been properly trained to start with, you'd never have a problem like that - forgetting what you are is at the core of it, you know. But, if he'd had shoddy training to start with or was a bred slave who'd probably had little or no formal training, it'd be worth the cost to enroll him in a reputable training program - something like the one I have down on the ranch. But, to get that sort of consideration, he'd have to be one damn fine looking stud with lots of years of service left in him, let me tell you."

"There's an answer for everything, it seems," I replied. "At least when it comes to slaves."

"I'm curious about Beauty's training," Joáo countered. "Rico's I know is good - I did it myself," he laughed. "That training will last a lifetime if you don't muck it up with a stupid owner. But Beauty I wonder about. He resisted just a tad when I milked him this morning and when I fucked him yesterday he wiggled around just a bit too much to tell me he'd had good training."

Beauty's eyes shot to the floor in shame and he shivered noticeably at the report from his master's guest.

"He was trained at a state slave training center in Kansas according to Will, his original owner. Of course, he was just 18 at the time but it seems to me that would make it all the better. Will never had a bit of trouble with him I know, nor have I," I added. "Why, aren't the state slave training centers any good in Kansas?"

"I have no idea. Did his last master tell you how long he was in that training center?" João pushed the issue.

"I think he said four months or so, maybe six - I can't remember. I could call him to find out if you think it's important, João."

"Don't bother, Christian. It's not the time as much as the quality of the program itself. Some government programs in Brazil are O.K. but some are just a joke - depends on which province. Some know exactly what they're doing - some don't. Maybe that's the case in the U.S. Ever heard of any problems of Kansas-trained slaves, Christian?" João asked with some concern.

"No, João, but I wouldn't hear that sort of thing anyway. It's not like I'm into buying slaves everyday, you know."

"I've got my sources. I'll check around before I leave. If the slave has been in a decent training program, that's one thing and you can relax. If he hasn't, I can take him back to Brazil on my plane and run him through my own training center and have him back to you within a month without a scar on his body and raring to go. I won't even charge you for it since you've proved to be a great host, Christian."

Beauty, hearing all of this, broke into tears without breaking position and tried to make sure his sobs were silent so as to not bring attention to himself. The horrors of the Kansas center just two years ago raced through his mind where he had entered a free-spirited teenage boy and left a broken slave nothing but property and eager to please anyone who bought him. He couldn't imagine a product of that program being anything but a good slave the rest of their life. But, then, he couldn't imagine Master João viewing him as suspect in his training just because he moaned a little when Master João forcibly fucked him and shuttered a little when Master João unexpectedly grabbed his balls in the kitchen and started pumping his big prick and massaging his balls until he shot off into the cup held in front of him. He had never resisted in any way or done anything but cooperate with the manhandling. After all, he was only a slave.

Beauty needn't have worried so much. Joáo made his calls and reported back the Kansas slave training center had a good reputation and reported few 'rouge' slaves among their alumni that ever needed to be retrained or disposed of.

"Sorry to have alarmed you, Christian, but I'm so used to slaves trained to Rico's standards I guess I'm overly critical of what other's are doing in the training arena."

"Hooray! Kansas is redeemed," I laughed and Beauty, still in full display, risked a relieved smile. "I had no intentions of being without Beauty for a month anyway while you worked him over at your ranch," I added. "He's too handy around here to be gone a whole month," I said as I reached over and rubbed Beauty's ass to emphasize what I was talking about. "But, if he ever needs retraining, I know where to send him - the same place as Rico was trained and the price you cited can't be beat."

Joáo left the next day in that he had done what he came to do and he needed to get back to his business he said. I could imagine how busy he probably was down in Brazil what with the constant arrival of new stock, the management of the huge operation he was running, and then constantly selling off his finished products before his holding pens were jammed.

"It's been three years since you visited my ranch, Christian," Joáo almost pleaded. "And we get along as well as ever despite being apart so long. It's like destiny has determined we're to be best friends forever. You don't seem overly occupied. Can't you come down for a good vacation before too long - you can even bring your slaves with you if you think you would miss them too much."

"It's not a bad idea, Joáo. I did really enjoy my last visit and you're a great host. And that ranch of yours has all sorts of hidden treats, so I can see why you're anxious to get back, business or not, you horny old bastard. I'll think on it and let you know if I can work something out."

"Be sure you do, Christian. I promise I won't drag you off to some slave dealers in Sao Paulo the next time like I did before. But, believe me, I never dreamed my friend Senor Alcazar was going off buying a few slaves when I set up the visit."

"That was one of the highlights of my trip, Joáo. If I do come down again, I'd love to visit some of the local markets - it's not only educational but fun."

"Whatever you want, buddy. As long as you visit, I'll set up anything you want - a bout with a fresh white stud from the rutting sheds; a romp with a muscular black from Africa; a good sucking by a fresh Middle Eastern boy - you name it, it's yours, my friend. But I think what you might really like is watching some fresh meat from right here in New York City being put through their paces as we turn them from the good-looking 'boy next door' to a high priced offering in next year's market place."

"You know me like a book, Joáo," I replied in a tone that told Joáo I would indeed seriously consider a visit in the near future.

Rico chauffeured us back to the New Jersey private air field with Beauty in the back sucking off Joáo so he would be completely drained before the six hour trip home alone.

"Have you ever traveled without a slave or two to play with?" I asked, rather worried about my friend's welfare. "I could loan you Beauty here for the trip if you'd promise to get him back to me before too long."

"That's nice of you, Christian, but not necessary. I've got a lot of paperwork to catch up on before I get back and can't afford the time to be distracted anyway. Besides, it's not like I've been deprived of any action while I was visiting you," he laughed as he put his hands around Beauty's head and pressed the boy's mouth totally into his groin and raised slightly out of the seat and gasped.

Joáo dumped a fresh load well down into Beauty's stomach just as we arrived at the private air facility. Joáo hopped onto the waiting plane and, within minutes, his plane could barely be seen in the sky.

"You drive, Beauty," I commanded. "I want Rico to suck me off on the way home. Joáo's not the only one needing a little relief."

"Yes, master," both slaves answered simultaneously as Beauty took the wheel and Rico took to the floor directly in front of me in the back seat, his mouth already open for action. By the time we arrived at my townhouse, I had been completely drained, Rico had had his afternoon snack, and Beauty was hard and dripping once again. We were back to normal.

CHAPTER 11

Two months later, I did arrange to visit João at his ranch. When I called him of my plans, he was wildly enthusiastic.

"It's a great time to visit. The weather's really nice this time of year and we're right in the middle of processing a huge new batch, Christian, that, if nothing else, are sure good to look at." João's excitement at the pending visit was reflected in the tone of his voice. "Are you bringing those two hunks of meat with you?" he asked.

"I don't think so, João. It's always a bother having them caged for shipment and it's not like I would need them down there - unless," I paused, "your hospitality isn't what it used to be?"

"I've got more than enough meat around the place to keep you well drained, Christian," João laughed, "if that's what you meant by hospitality."

"I was hoping to hear you say that, João. In that case, I'll just put them in the kennel while I'm gone. Those two would probably appreciate a little rest from their duties anyway," I responded.

"Make sure the kennel guarantees they'll exercise them regularly - you don't want them getting flabby while you're gone,"

João advised. "And make sure the kennel keeps them individually penned and that their wrists are chained to the cage bars when they're not being exercised. That way, they can't empty their balls and they'll be more than eager to see their master when you return."

Two hours later, João called back and said my timing was perfect. He had to deliver a dozen slaves to New York that had been purchased by a local trucking firm to load and unload their trucks. They weren't premium goods, he noted, but it would be cheaper to ship them up in his private jet than the usual airfreight arrangements. He planned on using the same air facility in New Jersey as before and the same Acme Moving delivery service to deliver the slaves from the plane to their new owner, also in Northern New Jersey. I could ride back in the plane and even bring my own two slaves with me if I wanted. "That way, Christian, it wouldn't cost you anything, you'll be a lot more comfortable than in a commercial plane, and it will take half the time. You'd have to change planes three times otherwise, as you know."

"Great," I answered. João gave me the estimated time of arrival and said the plane would start back the minute it refueled. "But, João, I think I'll still kennel my slaves. They'd just be in the way down at the ranch and, if you can make the trip with no slaves around as you did the last time you flew back from New York, I guess I can grin and bear it as well. Just have something for me to dump into when I get there," I snickered.

"Don't worry, Christian. You can fuck the chauffeur on the way to the ranch from the airport if you want - I can drive the damn car if you're that hard up." We both were laughing as we hung up.

The next day, I left Rico and Beauty at a reputable nearby kennel and, taking a cab, was in New Jersey at the designated time. João's sleek jet arrived exactly as scheduled and so did the Acme Moving agent. He promptly got the dozen slaves out of the aircraft's locked cages and out onto the tarmac where they stood in 'display' position before him the minute they saw the whip in his hand and a small bag of slave pellets in his other hand.

They were all big whites, deeply tanned, muscular, and young enough to guarantee several decades of hard work out of them. No one had bothered to body shave them, but their head hair was cut very short in the fashion of most draft slaves and their faces appeared to have been shaved at least weekly. All of them had some random whip scars on them, and none of them were by any stretch of the imagination handsome and none of them seemed to be particularly heavy hung. Their only clothing was a heavy iron collar with several attachment rings around their neck and a 'control' ring through the septum of their nose. No ear rings, no tit rings, no genital banding - all of these could get caught in equipment and damage the property. On the other hand, the nose ring was handy for securing them at night - any retaining chain in a wall at the warehouse would do - and it provided a good means of leashing them when they needed to be moved to another location or if they needed to be fixed in place. A 'control leash' fastened to a slave's nose ring was all that was necessary to insure a slave's almost complete cooperation with whatever his handler hand in mind.

"Their new owner has insured them for $75,000 each so whoever sold them must have made a neat little profit. Says on the bill of lading they're Australian - originally prisoners there before the wardens sold them off. But," he added, "that place in Brazil that bought them off the Australian wardens seemed to have done a decent job training them - they display well enough and certainly pay attention to the whip in my hand as well as these slave pellets I brought along," the Acme Moving agent laughed.

Addressing the slaves, he told them they had permission to piss in place which, with a sigh of relief they all did.

"All housebroken," the agents said with satisfaction. The agent then had them turn around and noted there was no shit on their rump.

"The place in Brazil must have flushed them out good in preparation for the trip so they can hold it until we get them to their new home."

When the slaves had finished emptying their bladders as ordered, the agent threw each of them a slave pellet which was quickly swallowed with the expected, "Thank you, master."

"As you boys probably know by now, the only way you're going to keep from being hungry all the time is to do exactly as you're told - promptly and with a big smile on your ugly faces."

"Yes, master," the 12 answered in unison, never taking their eyes off of the small bag of slave pellets in his hand.

"Now get your ugly asses into a cage in that truck over there - one to a cage and back into them so your head is up against the cage door - sooner you've tucked yourself in properly, the sooner you'll have another pellet of slave chow to chew on along with a nice drink of water."

"Yes, master," they all chorused in unison as they clamored to fulfill the command.

"I know where they're going, sir," the agent said in explanation, although he owed me none. "From now on, they'll be feed a piece of slave chow at a time - when they perform exceptionally well - and they'll earn a sip of water the same way. They never fed them regularly. Each scrap of food and every drop of water has to be earned from now on. It means their overseers have to carry around bags of slave pellets and a water bottle, but they claim they get more work out of them that way. I could see where it would work, though. Nothing like an empty belly and a dry mouth to really motivate a slave."

"I hear some owners get much the same results by only allowing slaves sexual relief as a reward for exceptionally hard work. Of course, that would only work if the slaves were still young and randy and you restrained them enough so they couldn't relieve themselves on their own or with each other."

"That's the system Acme Moving uses with their warehouse slaves in that they want the overseers free to discipline the slaves with their whips and prods and you can't do that well if you're always having to feed and water them. The problem is, sir, you hate to get around those slaves - they're always hard and dripping and it gets messy if you rub up against them. I've even seen them rubbing up against a warehouse pole trying to get off before the overseer whips them off it. In fact, sir, some of them start humping each other if they think the overseer is dosing or taking a leak himself."

"Sounds like either way of insuring good work output has its good and bad points," I responded. "Someday they'll probably work out some combination of the two that works best."

"Let me check out the inside of the plane before you get in, sir," the agent said. "I just want to make sure the slaves didn't crap or piss in there. If so, by God, they're going to clean it up in that I'm sure they were told not to. But you know slaves, sir."

The agent went up the stairs and looked around briefly from the cabin door, sniffing the air as he did so.

"Some body smell from slave sweat, but it'll soon go away. Otherwise, nice and clean, sir. I don't think those Aussie slaves let one drop of piss out of their bodies. Well disciplined lot, it looks like," the agent said, obviously pleased. "I shouldn't have any trouble with them getting them to their new home."

With that, he proceeded to lock the individual cage doors inside his delivery truck and I got on Joáo's private jet which, if you didn't mind looking at the stainless steel cages inside, was nicely fitted out - luxurious leather lounge chairs, tables for your drinks, a fold-down 'fucking bench' in soft plastic, a neat little refrigerator with lots of ice in the built-in bar, reading lamps, cabin air-conditioning controls, and an assortment of the latest magazines which would be of interest to Joáo, e.g., "The Slave Marketeer;" "Modern Slave Training;" and "Slave Breeding." All had a world-wide subscription base, I realized, but I'd never taken the time to actually read through a whole issue. Now, I figured, I would have that time.

As the plane took off, I began thumbing through the latest issue of "The Slave Marketeer." It proved so interesting I barely had time to start in on "Slave Breeding" which was equally interesting before the plane started to land in Campinas. I had heard these magazines sold as well to those not in the slave business as to those in it. After reading the two issues I got through, I could see why. It was damn interesting reading and the Slave Marketeer ran a full-page ad from the very place I was headed - Joáo's ranch.

Joáo was right there to meet me as he had promised and one of the two slaves he had in tow got my luggage off his private jet and into the back of Joáo's Range Rover. Both the slaves he had with him were fantastic beauties - one an olive-skinned well muscled boy with prodigious equipment Joáo claimed was Italian; the other a smooth skinned brown boy with nicely developed pecs and huge nipples from a breeding farm in Senegal Joáo had picked up somewhere. Both slaves would be labeled 'prime' in any market in the world. I had just read in "The Slave Marketeer" that the 'prime' label was only given to about one slave out of a thousand -

even today when breeding was rapidly eliminating so-called 'trash stock.' These two slaves were certainly in that one in a thousand category.

"Take your pick, Christian," João laughed as he saw me looking the two slaves over. "One can drive while you fuck the other. Then, they can switch and the other one can suck me off."

"Sounds good, João. I'll take the Italian boy but right now, I'd like a good suck rather than fucking him here in the Rover. A little cramped for a good fuck. By the way, João, I read a few of those magazines you had in the plane and saw your ad in 'The Slave Marketeer.' Very nice presentation. Made me want to lift up the phone and order a lot of slaves from you."

"That's the feedback I like to hear, Christian. But let me tell you, that Italian that's going to service you on the way home puts the stock in the ad to shame."

"Well, the brown boy from Senegal or wherever isn't exactly hard on the eyes," I laughed as I pointed to the big bulge tenting out from my loose slacks.

"That's what they're here for, Christian. And the best part is, they know it!" João laughed as he got up in front with the naked Senegalese boy and I got in the back with the Italian slave already digging my prick out of my pants with his beautifully shaped mouth already open for action.

"I see what you mean about knowing why they're here," I laughed as, with one movement, the Italian slave engulfed my entire organ and I felt his throat muscles wrap tightly around my shaft. I marveled at the slave's long eyelashes, his flashing black eyes smiling up at me, and his dark skin as smooth as butter. The slave literally purred as I ran one hand through his head of soft black ringlets and massaged his large dark brown nipples with my other.

"Jesus Christ, João," I gasped. "Is this a slave or some sort of milking machine?"

"Both," João laughed as the brown chauffeur moved the car out onto the main road while his owner started playing with his ringed nipples and his huge banded genitals.

"Where did you find this treasure" I gasped as the slave slid his clenched mouth up and down my shaft, showing no difficulties in taking me completely down his throat without the usual natural gagging and choking.

"One of my agents bought him at an orphanage in an impoverished area of southern Italy. The priest running the place was overjoyed to get the $100,000 'donation' my agent gave him for the 19-year-old 'ward.' To make it all nice and legal, the priest called it an "adoption fee" and we went along with it as long as the priest signed the full ownership papers we demand with any purchase. The priest just had one stipulation - that the boy be brought up Catholic. We assured him he would be shipped to a Catholic country and his new owner was Catholic himself who gave generously to the church, but, unfortunately, we didn't offer slaves religious training. We did, in all honesty, point out the boy would probably be used sexually - slaves as good looking as he was could expect nothing less. The priest's reply? "It's in God's hands," as he gave his blessing to the handsome orphan he had just sold. The priest then proceeded to try and sell my agent several other late teenagers just blossoming into full manhood."

"I'm being sucked off by a slave officially blessed by a priest?" I chuckled as the beautiful boy worked his mouth up and down my shaft expertly.

"That's what my agent said," Joáo laughed. "I wonder if I should ask my parish priest to come out and sanctify the Catholic boys I'm selling off each and every day? You think I could raise their price if I advertised them as 'sanctified with a special commission for their new life by the local priest.' My priest would do it if I made it a stipulation for my next big donation. Christian? You're Catholic along with me. Are all religions this.. well.. hypocritical? Shit, blessing slaves before their sale implying it's God's Will or it wouldn't be happening!"

"Joáo, maybe the priests are right. It just might be God's Will. They end up slaves, don't they, and it's not just random chance. Besides, Joáo, all religions preach one thing and practice another on some issues - they've got a responsibility to adjust to the needs of society just like everything else - look at the Mormons, one man to every four women and suddenly polygamy is part of the religion. Look at the non-Catholic countries - they embraced slavery just like the Catholic countries - no difference. And look at countries that are non-Christian - they buy and sell slaves just like the Christian countries - no difference. So if it makes that old priest in Italy feel better to bless the boy he was selling into slavery, what difference does it make? It doesn't change the new slave's life one way or the other - see, he's sucking my dick like his life depends on draining me dry."

"Well, Christian, before you justify everything so cozily, my agent informed me in checking the boy out before purchase that he found he was far from virgin. In fact, he told me, the boy was well used to being fucked when he bought him. Now just who do you think was fucking this handsome boy so regularly?"

"No one but the Vatican claims priests aren't men first and priests second. Look at your slave, Joáo. Who could resist something like this?"

This conversation was typical of the bond between Joáo and me, I reflected. I could see Joáo was the same person he had always been and my visit was going to be pleasurable as well as interesting.

As the Italian slave really got to work, I had forgotten all about Rico and Beauty back at the New York kennel with their handcuffs locked to the cage bars to make sure their balls were full when I returned.

CHAPTER 12

I was surprised at all the changes in the Campinas area since my last visit just a few years earlier. There was no doubt now that Brazil was a full slave economy. Slaves seem to have monopolized all types of occupations, everything from farming (as one would certainly expect) to building new roads and buildings (again certainly to be expected). These activities in New York were entirely slave powered as well by now. But in the Campinas area, trucks and busses had been largely replaced by wagons pulled by teams of slaves in full harness, taxis by slave-pulled rickshaws, and, rather spectacularly, limousines and private cars by rather gaudy litters carried on the shoulders of very muscular litter bearers. It was obvious Brazilians were cutting their dependence on paid labor and traditional fuels to a minimum.

When I mentioned this to João, he said fuel costs had risen to the point where it was now considerably cheaper to convert to slave power. The cost of a team of slaves and the cost of feeding them was now about one-third of what methanol cost (Brazilians had long ago learned to make methanol from sugar cane) for any given usage. People had adjusted to the disadvantages of using slaves: each team generally required a whipmaster, himself a slave, to get full output consistently; it was obviously slower, especially in intercity transit; and slave shit on the roads was a problem sometimes. On the other hand, a nice litter could be showier than a luxury car if done right and, with traffic congestion the way it was, it was often faster to go by litter and especially rickshaw than in the cabs and cars of old.

"It's certainly been good for my bottom line," Joáo commented. "The price of slaves has almost doubled since methanol got so expensive and the demand for slaves goes up every day it seems. It's hard to keep a nice inventory on hand anymore the way the pens empty at each sale."

I studied the scores of litters we passed. Most owners had carefully sought out a 'matched' team for their litter, i.e., all the slave bearers were about the same height, the same skin color, the same very muscular build, and, in many cases, were obviously matched in genital size. Owners had a clear-cut preference toward bearers with large, circumcised organs that protruded well with a tight-fitting genital band. Each bearer was invariably 'fastened' to the litter in some way whether it was a short chain linking his collar to the litter, a tight chain from a tit ring, or a taut leash from a genital band. That way the slave looked like he was a part of the litter itself, there was no way to escape from the litter, and it assured the slave lifted and lowered the litter smoothly and gently to avoid being choked or having his tits pulled or his balls squeezed most painfully. Many owners had matched the slaves so carefully they looked close to clones, especially when all were fully body shaved and worked nude. I shared my admiration at these studied displays with Joáo.

"You generally have to search a number of markets to match a full team closely and be willing to pay what it takes to get what's needed. It's been a real boon in selling off brothers who look a lot alike, and half-brothers sharing the same stud sire from the breeding farms. And muscular twins strong enough to serve as litter bearers are selling at great prices once the demand for matched teams started developing."

"And nice for brothers up for sale," I added. "That way they have a chance of staying together if they look a lot alike. I suppose those newly enslaved prefer to be around family if they can."

"Well, they just might, Christian," João laughed, "but you're such a sentimentalist you're absolutely charming in that your perceptions are so out-of-touch with the realities of slavery. Even if you get sold with your brother to an owner, the odds of both of you staying with that same owner over the years is practically nil. I don't think any owner I know of even thinks about that when he buys or sells a slave - they're just property and family is a concept that only has any meaning if you are free. Once you're a slave, your owner is the closest thing you have to a family. Those two slaves of yours, Beauty and Rico, think of you as their father until you sell them and they get another father. After all, like their father before they were enslaved, you make all the decisions; you decide what they do and don't do; and you can sell them when you feel like it. But you also feed and house them; you protect them from predators and kidnapers; and you fix them up if they get injured. That's the security of a family from a slave's viewpoint. That's why most slaves are quite devoted and damn loyal to their masters."

We passed a 18-wheel wagon, as big as any semi in the old days, being pulled by a team of 20 slaves, 10 reined on each side of the long hitch out in front with a whipmaster busily making sure all the slaves were in step to the pace of a drum manned by a small boy five or six years old who didn't weigh much. The carefully choreographed movements assured a smooth, rapid pace down the road. The whip quickly found its mark on the back and rump of any slave who was out of step with the others or failed to keep up with the fast pace of the drum, no matter how much they were panting or dripping with sweat. I was amazed at how fast the wagon was actually moving considering the power source and commented as such to João.

"All those big high pressure tires on the wagon have a lot to do with it," João said professionally, "along with good lubrication on the ball bearings. If you have enough good strong slaves hitched up, like that wagon does, the only limitation as to speed are the lungs of the slaves. No matter how much you beat them, at a certain point, they simply can't exchange more oxygen in those lungs than nature allows. A good whipmaster keeps a slave right at the maximum exchange rate the entire time he's in rein. Just short of passing out and slack enough to assure endurance for an all-day run - the slave's only problem that way is that his lungs burn like hell for several hours after he's unhitched."

I marveled at how educational this trip was proving to be and how much we Americans had to learn yet about effective use of slaves.

Just then, João's Senegalese slave chauffeur brought the Range Rover to a quick stop. There was a disturbance on the road ahead. Much to his credit, the Italian slave never wavered from his assigned duty and kept my shaft completely down his throat as he continued to suckle me.

I lowered the window to hear, "Rogue slave! Rogue slave!" from a man standing by the road, obviously bemused by what was going on, whatever it was.

"What's a rogue slave?" I asked João as I saw a handsome young rickshaw slave, chained by his wrists to the rickshaw's shaft, straining to get loose and screaming at the top of his lungs as he rocked the rickshaw around violently in his efforts to free himself..

"Listen," João advised as he too lowered his window to hear the commotion.

"You God damn son-of-a-bitch," the slave screamed as his throat muscles pushed out bright red against his tight slave collar. "I'm not an animal - I'm not an animal! You're treating me worse than an animal, you bastard. Even a horse isn't fucked in public like this, you God damned pervert. You can't treat me like this, you fucking asshole. You...."

The slave's soliloquy abruptly ended as a long penis gag was forced down the slave's throat and tightly strapped around his head by the police who had quickly arrived because of the traffic holdup. With a rain of whip blows that covered the slave's body with blood, the police drove the errant slave and his rickshaw over to the side of the road so traffic could continue.

"What happened, João?" I asked as the traffic began to creep forward again.

"That's what's called a rogue slave, Christian. A slave that goes berserk and forgets what he or she is. In this particular case, I would guess little to no training or a patently inept training program. That slave doesn't even know he's a slave obviously. He was probably free just a week or so ago would be my hunch and some guy bought him for rickshaw duty assuming he was fully broken and trained for his new role in life. One of three things will happen, probably depending on how much he sold for. One, he could be sent off for rendering and the owner will just cut his loss. Two, he'll be returned to whoever sold him to his owner for a rebate and retraining. Three, the owner will train him in place restrained by his wrists to the rickshaw, which shouldn't take too long with heavy use of the electric prod, unbridled use of the bull whip, food and water deprivation during the entire retraining time, and continual adjustment counseling. Four, the owner will try to sell him off to some unsuspecting rube at a heavily discounted price." With that, Joáo jumped out of the car and walked over to the irate owner, a young man looking to be no more than 19 or 20.

"Went rogue on you, my friend?" Joáo said soothingly as he ran his hand through the bound slave's hair.

"Did you hear what came out of that slave's mouth?" the owner said, still red in the face from his anger. "That will never happen again. As soon as we're home, I'll have my handler mute the bastard and after that his opinions will be kept to himself."

"I heard the animal part, my friend," Joáo said. Turning to the gagged slave, he jerked his face upwards with his head hair and said, "Of course you're an animal - all slaves are. Whatever gave you the silly idea you weren't an animal now? And even though horses generally aren't fucked in public here in Brazil that I know of, slaves certainly are at every opportunity. It's good for them - teaches them their position in life, especially when it's done in public, and, of course, it's a good opportunity for them to serve their master over and above merely pulling their rickshaw to the very limits of their body. It's a compliment to be fucked by your master or any one your master allows to fuck you. It gives you a way to thank your owner for feeding you and keeping you away from the slave rendering plants."

Joáo looked at the owner who was obviously relieved someone else was temporally dealing with the rogue slave and continued stroking the restrained slave, moving his hand down to the slave's banded sexual organs and stroking the slave until he was hard and dripping.

"You won't be able to talk anymore after the handler has burnt out your vocal cords, and you'll learn to appreciate the food and water your owner provides after a good five days of no slave chow and a full 72 hours of no water" - nodding to the owner to make sure he understood the prescription - "and 50 lashes of the bull whip by the handler is always instructive for a new slave like yourself who's confused and uncertain of his new status." João again nodded to the owner to make sure he understood the necessity of the murderous whipping which would leave the slave unable to work for several days, his body permanently scarred, but rather permanently changed in attitude. "And having a 12 x 5 dildo up your ass, held in by a good tight dildo holder, for a couple of months, will teach you your ass is property of your owner, just like the rest of you, and is there to be used by your master, whenever or however he wants, including right here in the streets if that's what he wants. In fact, many rickshaw slaves are fitted with a dildo every time they're harnessed in place just to remind them they're slaves and always will be," again nodding to the slave's owner who shook his head in his understanding of the necessity of the prescribed measures.

"Once these corrective measures are taken, with your adjustment to your new status in life paramount in the concerns of your new owner, and you take on a healthy perspective of your new role in life now that you're a valuable slave property, you'll forget all about this foolishness today and carve out the best life you can for yourself. Look around, slave. Everyone is laughing at how foolish you've been."

The slave did look up at the crowd gathered around the rickshaw and burst into tears and sobs muffled by his penis gag.

"See, I knew you'd be ashamed of all the trouble you've caused," his anguish was deliberately misinterpreted by João. Taking a huge plastic dildo out of the Range Rover, João proceeded to work it slowly up the slave's ass who wiggled and groaned but couldn't move due to his wrist restraints on the rickshaw's shafts. The slave's eyes turned white with pain at the invasion.

"A good fucking, right here in public, is always soothing," João announced to the slave, continuing to pump the slave's erect shaft as he worked the dildo deeply into the boy's ass. "I can't imagine a slave not liking a good fucking. See, you're prick shows you're enjoying it - it's all hard and dripping already."

After a few minutes, the slave squirted a full load onto the pavement beneath him right in front of everyone and, as his body relaxed in response to the orgasm, the fight seemed to go out of him for the time being and, after João had retrieved his huge 'training' dildo, the police led the slave back to the stables at his owner's house where he could be muted, beaten, starved, and fucked into permanent submission.

But not before the owner profusely thanked João for his being such a "Good Samaritan" and for his excellent advice in how to remedy a bad situation. Little did that rickshaw owner realize he was talking to one of Brazil's leading experts in slave breaking.

"Will those remedies really work?" I asked João as the brown chauffeur got the Range Rover up to full speed again and João was again churning that slave's balls for his amusement.

"Should, if he follows my advice completely," João said with some satisfaction. "If it doesn't, he knows what to do."

"What's that, João?" I asked out of curiosity.

"Well, I gave him my card. He could send the slave to my center for retraining for a hefty fee. Or," he laughed, "he could send him to the rendering plant. The slave's hide won't bring much after 50 lashes of a bull whip - it will be too scared up to be worth anything - but his organs should bring a decent return - about 10% of what he probably paid for the slave, but it beats nothing at all."

Two hours later, we were on João's property and began the long drive from the highway to his manor house and, beyond that, his processing and training centers, his holding pens, and his sales venues. By this time, João and I both had been completely drained by the well-trained slaves, a feat accomplished by switching chauffeurs half way there during a rest break where the slaves were watered and allowed to piss. That allowed me to compare the striking Senegalese boy to the Italian in their sucking skills and allowed João to fuck the Italian in the back of the Range Rover once he had the beauteous olive-skinned slave put down all the seats back there.

I was getting as bad as João, I thought to myself as I looked down on the beautiful brown slave who had just serviced me. Three times today I had been drained: once by Rico; once by the Italian; and now by the Senegalese.

At this rate, I'd be worn out by the time by the time I was 35, no different than male brothel slaves, who were usually 'dried up' by the time they reached their 30th birthday. Who said slaves weren't addictive? And harmful to your health if you didn't watch it!

Joáo's manor house was as comfortable as usual, with the air-conditioning just right, the decor tasteful, and gorgeous naked slaveboys always available to assist but never obtrusive. I was shown to one of the several guest suites which had been recently remodeled. Now there were true suites that included a sitting room/study; a huge bedroom; a walk-in closet; a luxurious bath complete with separate tub, shower and bidet and, adjoining, an unobtrusive slave cell complete with its own shower, enema, grooming, and lubrication facilities. Even the accouterments handy in a sidebar were carefully thought out for the guests' convenience: whips of various types; a huge assortment of dildos, butt plugs and tails, leashes of varying lengths and styles; battery operated electric prods; along with the usual restraints useful with slaves - handcuffs, choke collars, tit pincers, and ball holders to mention a few.

I took a quick shower and threw on some fresh clothes before I started exploring the suite. In the slave cell, which I hadn't even noticed before my bath, I found a well tanned white slave kneeling quietly with his knees wide apart to best display his impressive large endowment. He was totally body shaved outside his nice fine black head hair, had sparkling blue eyes once he raised his head at my command, and the creamiest smooth skin I'd ever seen on a full-grown man. He wore a thick leather collar in bright red with brass grommets, 2" brass rings in each large tit; and a matching brass band tightly fitted around his sexual organs.

"What have we here?" I asked the slave whose eyes were cast down properly.

"Jim, Master, here for your pleasure," he answered in a deep bass voice that was so masculine it seemed to emanate from his balls.

"And where were you from originally, Jim?" I asked.

"Oklahoma, Master, in the United States," the handsome slave answered.

"Were you bred there, or have you been sold into slavery?" I asked.

"Master, I'm not off a breeding farm, although we have those in Oklahoma now, Master. I was in the career Army, Master, but went A.W.O.L. in protest to the war. When I was caught trying to cross the border into Mexico, the Army sold me into slavery under the standard provisions of the National Security Act, and I ended up here in Brazil for my slave conditioning and specialized training, Master. Once I was down here, I was two months in basic training and another two months in special sex training, Master."

"And how did that go, Jim?" I asked, delighted with his easy, unassuming conversational style.

"About like the Army, Master. Not much different, really, outside the specialized training and the fact we were never issued any uniforms but our birthday suits and my collar, these tit rings, and my genital band. Of course, Master, the Army didn't brand and tattoo us, but I like that better than always having those damn dog tags jingling around my neck. And, here it's so damn hot outside, I didn't mind not having clothes, especially when none of the other guys did either, Master."

"A slave with a body like yours should be proud to show it all for his owner," I commented, "especially with a nice big prick like yours, slave."

"Of course, Master," the slave answered promptly.

"Well, I see your point, Jim. 'Master' instead of 'Sir;' a slave collar instead of dog tags; a chance to display your body instead of an uncomfortable uniform. What the hell! And following orders and living a life laid out by others is just like the Army, isn't it, Jim?"

"Yes, Master. Except I feel more appreciated here than I ever did in the Army, master."

"Then, Jim, you're pretty happy with the way things turned out?"

"Yes, Master," Jim said as he boldly looked up and winked at me invitingly. "Especially, Master, since I got chosen to be a sex slave. The Army didn't offer that specialty that I was aware of and, once you settle in and get use to it, some of the time it can prove to be downright fun - even for the slave."

"Well, Jim, a slave is usually on the receiving end of things," I laughed. "And the main job, as you no doubt are fully aware, is to make the master happy, not you."

"Of course, Master. But a randy young buck like myself still enjoys a good romp no matter whose calling the shots," Jim said smiling. "I get a lot more action now by a hundred times than I ever got in the Army, Master," Jim added, "despite the R & R and the Army whore houses."

"Yes, Jim, but wasn't that all straight sex?" I asked, "and here you're forced into servicing male masters for the main part?"

"Yes, master. But, Master, that's the glory of it. I wasn't straight to start with although I can bed a wench down with the best of them if that's what I'm ordered to do. Being a sex slave is the best thing that ever happened to me, Master, and I'm going to make sure no master is unhappy with this boy in his bed." He paused a bit and than added, "or a mistress either if that's what is needed. But a master would be even better," the slave licked his lips and again risked giving me an inviting look.

"Prove it, Jim," I said as I unlocked his cell door and, taking him by his collar, led him over to the bed.

As soon as I had slid out of my clothes and was up on the bed myself, Jim did indeed prove himself to my complete satisfaction and then some. I forgot all about joining my host for supper or evening entertainment and it was morning before I emerged from the suite, freshly bathed and even dressed by my new suite slave, Jim, who had proven himself inexhaustible. I had fucked him on his back with his legs thrown over my shoulders, on his hands and knees with his knees spread wide apart, standing bent over with his legs spread apart, and on his knees with his mouth spread wide for my entry.

When I was deep up his ass, I asked him about any family before he was sold off.

"Slaves don't have families, Master," the body beneath me gasped as I pumped vigorously into him.

"Of course not, slave, and how dare you presume to lecture a master," I shot back harshly, slapping him soundly across the face. "I said before you were sold into slavery, slave," using the word slave instead of his name to indicate my irritation.

"Sorry, Master," Jim said humbly as he noticeably pushed back to take more of me into him, trying to convince me of his total submission. "They disowned me when I went A.W.O.L. and

I think they're the ones who tipped the National Security Forces as to where I was, Master."

"No matter. As you said, slaves don't have families," I replied as I arched my back and shot deep into him and then had him clean my prick off with his tongue of the juices, lubricants, and cum that was all over it by this time.

When João joined me for breakfast, he asked whether the slave in my suite had proven to be satisfactory.

"The Oklahoma Wonder?" I smiled. "That slave is simply priceless."

"I thought you'd like him," João smiled. "You're into those Midwestern corn-fed types."

"Did you know he's gay?" I asked João.

"No, I suspected as much as he took to his training with zeal. It doesn't make any difference, though, Christian..." João started his lecture.

"I know straight slaves can service you just as well with good training, João," I interrupted. "Nevertheless, Jim is a natural as a sex slave - and, I would argue, noticeably better than either Beauty or Rico, who are straight left to their own devices as far as I know."

"Now you're not going to be happy with them when you get back to New York, despite their long wait in the kennels without a single chance to unload," João laughed. "Maybe, if you're real nice to me, Christian, I'll give you Jim to take home with you as a parting gift."

"No gifts, João. You promised. And besides," I laughed, "I fully intend to have Jim so worn out by the time I leave, with your permission of course, you'll be considering selling him off with a lot of old brothel slaves just to recoup a little of what he must have cost you."

"Oh! Christian. Jim didn't cost me much. The National Security agency in the U.S. sells off their prisoners ridiculously cheap. It's practically like they pay you to get rid of their 'terrorists.'"

"He's a 'terror' all right. That boy would make anyone forget about politics," I laughed. "But, if he came to you cheap and he didn't take all that long to train, I will be more than eager to buy him from you. We agreed to no gifts and I can fully afford, as you know, to buy a boy I really enjoy."

"Well, I'll sell him to you then." João stepped over to his computer and checked some files.

"He only cost me $50,000 and his training and upkeep cost me about $20,000. Allow me my usual 30% markup and I'm making plenty charging you $100,000 although I admit a boy like that in New York would set you back twice that much."

"Sold, João," I said as I handed him my credit card. "Put it on Visa now and I won't have to worry about paying you later."

"That's fine," João said swiping my card through his machine. "But I insist on paying his upkeep as long as you're my guest here."

"That I'll let you do, João. The slave chow shouldn't cost you more than a dollar a day or so - I know that's about what it cost me to feed Beauty and Rico each. And, can I keep his collar, tit rings, and genital band? They all fit well now."

"When I sell a slave, it's as is - that's includes whatever fittings he's got. I even throw in a tube or two of lubricant if they're worth fucking."

"Then I want four or five tubes, João," I joked as João went to a nearby closet and lugged out a full case of K-Y to give me.

"This should last you through your stay, my ruttish friend," João laughed. "Welcome to Brazil."

I thought back to the rogue slave as well as Jim, my new property and my face clouded over briefly.

"What's wrong, Christian," João asked, genuinely concerned.

"That rogue slave we saw coming up here, João - his owner was just a teenager, it seemed, and he must have been, well, old enough to be his owner's father practically. And I must look like a kid to Jim - he must be 28 or so and I'm, well, you know. Isn't it hard for a slave to respect a master who is just a kid compared to them?"

"Why should it, Christian?" João replied, obviously puzzled. "One's a master; one's a slave. One's property of the other. What does age have to do with it. Respect is an entitlement when you own a property, whatever its age."

"But how does a mature slave feel being under the yoke of a teenage kid, like that rickshaw slave back there?"

"Who gives a shit how a slave 'feels' about something or other? Jesus, Christian, you think up the silliest damn things I ever heard of. Think of all the prime age slaves given as gifts to teenagers by their mothers and fathers. Or all those slaves given as awards to young kids winning this and that? They all get fucked silly if they're even halfway decent looking. Do you think anyone ever thought about the fact the slave is older and more grown up than their master? It's totally irrelevant. A slave is obligated to serve his master or mistress and that goes whether their owner is 5 or 50. Slaves know that! Why can't you? Age has nothing to do with it. Ownership has everything to do with it. If you're the property of someone else, then you damn well better respect them. Remember that, Christian," João laughed, "if you ever get yourself enslaved somehow and find yourself sold off to a 12-year-old boy with pimples on his face and who's so young he can't even get it up yet. He's still the master and you're still the slave."

"Yes, but Jim must wonder a little about being fucked at the whim of someone a lot younger than him," I persisted.

"He better not be, Christian, or its back to the training sheds for him. But I noticed your great concern for a slave's feelings didn't extend over to buying outright a slave who doesn't have a clue he's changing hands. How does the slave feel about being sold without even knowing about it? What if he doesn't want to be sold?"

"I hadn't thought about it, João," I admitted.

"Oh! Don't worry about it. When he does find out, he'll probably be delirious with joy with his good fortune in not being sold yet to a 70 year old mistress fat and ugly as sin. That's the usual fate of slave's like him, you know. Most sex slaves are sold off to those who have to buy their bed partners anymore - no free person would dream of having sex with them. If you do eventually ask him about what he thinks about getting sold to you, I'm sure he'll tell you how tickled he is at his good luck. But, Christian, that too is totally irrelevant. No one, including slaves, values the opinions of slaves. Slaves aren't entitled to feelings, thoughts, or opinions about what happens to them. That's one of the first things they learn after they're enslaved. What I'm saying, Christian, that if you asked Jim such a stupid question, he would think you were crazy or something and, I'm sure, wouldn't even know how to answer such a dumb question."

Nevertheless, I did ask Jim the "dumb" question when I was fucking him on his back that next night, his huge prick hard and dripping pressed against my stomach as I plowed into him. As Joáo had predicted, he just stared at me a while, unable to even understand what the question was it was so out of a slave's realm of cognition.

"Sorry, master, I don't understand," he responded - honestly, I thought.

I was learning here in Brazil. I never asked such a 'dumb' question again.

CHAPTER 13

The next few days were a whirlwind of activity. Joáo was proud of his ranch and wanted me to see it all, although he thought I would most enjoy seeing the basic training center for his purchases who had been newly enslaved, his sex training facility where my own new purchase Jim had received his special training, and the training facility for those destined to be eventually sold as rickshaw and drayage slaves. Each would warrant at least a few hours, Joáo told me, but he was sure I would find it interesting.

"Could we visit your breeding facility, Joáo?" I asked.

"Of course, Christian," Joáo replied, "but outside of watching two slaves rut, there's not much to see. But you might enjoy looking the studs over that we're currently using. Some mighty impressive boys in the pens back there, if I do say so myself."

"Could we start with where Jim was trained?" I asked.

"The basic training or the sex training?" Joáo said.

"The sex training," I replied. "I've always wondered how they got a slave up to market standards in that area."

"Oh, there's no mystery to it, Christian, as you'll see in a few minutes if that's where you want to start."

"I do, but I don't want to take so much of your time, João. I know you've got a business to run. Why don't I take my new slave Jim with me and he can explain it to me - after all, he's a recent graduate I understand. If he can't explain what's going on, I don't know who could. And you'd get a chance to catch up on some of your paperwork while we're gone, João."

"That's considerate of you, Christian. That place is pretty self-explanatory anyway and Jim should be able to any questions you have - he is a recent alumni, as you say."

"When we get back, maybe you could show me the rickshaw training center or whatever you called it, João. I'm real interested after seeing that 'rogue slave' the other day."

"Be glad to, and once you see that operation, I think you can see where it was obvious that rogue never had any real training for his new job," João laughed.

With that, João went to his office to catch up on some work and I went back to my suite where Jim was busily completing his two hours of mandatory daily calisthenics specifically designed to keep his body in prime shape and limber for a master's use. He was covered in sweat and still panting a bit when I arrived. He thought I wanted to use him then and there, quickly assuming a slave's submission position on his hands and knees with his legs spread wide to expose the puckered opening of his asshole.

"Master," he panted, obviously expecting to be fucked.

"Not so eager, Jim," I chuckled. "Take a clean shower, oil your body, and get your ass back here pronto. I want to take you to your old stomping grounds."

"Yes, Master," Jim choked out, a look of complete failure on his face as he headed for the bathroom in accordance with my command.

When he returned within minutes, his body agleam, I hooked a short walking leash to his genital ring and we started on the short journey to the nearby facility.

"Why do you look so... well.. so heartbroken, Jim? Aren't you proud to accompany your master when he takes a stroll?"

"Oh, yes, master, but... but are you returning me for retraining, master? I had hoped... master.... that I was proving satisfactory to you, master. I'm sorry, master, that I haven't pleased you," he said apologetically as I led him down the sidewalk literally by his balls.

I jerked his leash sharply to show my irritation and the slave gasped from the pain in his balls.

"You stupid asshole," I laughed. "Master Joáo was too busy to take me on a tour of the sex training facility right now and I suggested you should be able to give me a decent tour since you graduated from the place just a few weeks ago, unless," I paused, "you think you need some retraining, Jim."

I look of relief swept over the handsome slave's face and he adjusted his pace since I had shortened his leash, forcing him to keep exact step with me to keep his balls from being stretched continually.

"Thank you for this honor, master, and, 'no,' I don't think I need retraining quite this soon, master, although, of course, that's not a slave's decision, master."

"One slip-up, Jim, and that's where you'll be. You know that and it's always good to keep that in mind. No master, including me, will tolerate a slave who is not giving everything they've been trained to do... and more," I replied adamantly.

"Yes, master," Jim replied as we entered his former 'home' during a two month stretch.

The trainers, all slaves themselves, promptly knelt with their heads bowed when they spotted a master. When I told them I was Master Joáo's guest and was here for a visit with my new purchase as my guide, they relaxed and, with a nod of dismissal from me, went back to their work.

"Hey, guys, look who's here," the trainers yelled to others in the next room. "Jim's brought his new owner over for a look-see." They nodded to Jim with satisfaction, proud that their recent trainee had found a new owner so fast and that he was being honored by being allowed to show the facility to his new master.

"His new master must be impressed with the slave," I overheard one of them say to another. "We must have done a good job on him," another said while still another said, "Jim must have learned his sex lessons well to be honored like that by his new owner." Still another commented, "I told him that big prick of his would find a buyer." I chuckled at the last comment since every trainer in the place seemed to be equally well endowed.

The place itself was large and impressive. On one side, at least 25 trainees, all very good looking and well equipped, were forced on their knees by tight thigh restraints, vigorously sucking their trainers, who had their hands gripping their charges' heads to guide them through the process. No matter how much the trainees choked and gagged as the trainers' huge pricks were being forced down the trainers' throats, the trainers held them steady until their pricks were well down the trainees' throats and practically into their stomachs as one after another, they discharged a full load down a suckling throat.

On the other side, another 25 were chained in place on rutting benches which forced their legs wide apart, their arms above them, and their ass hole completely accessible. Mounting each were another 25 trainers, all hugely equipped themselves, who were pumping in and out of those holes slowly but deeply as the slaves beneath them gasped, groaned, and tried to wiggle their butts to lessen the pain by opening up more.

"How long are they fucked like this?" I asked Jim.

"All day, master," Jim answered.

When I looked surprised, he explained.

"Those on the rutting benches get fresh lube, a chance to stretch, and a new trainer every half hour, master. Those on their knees get an opportunity to walk around a bit and a drink of water each time they swallow another load and before a new prick is presented to their mouth."

"Jesus, that's solid training," I commented.

"Yes, master. By the end of a training day, your stomach is full of cum if you're on the right side and your ass is mighty sore if you're on the left side. The next day, you're switched to the other side. Back and forth until a slave shows he can handle it with no sweat, Master."

"And how long is that, Jim?"

"After a month, it's just routine and you can't remember when you weren't sucking dick or taking it up the ass, Master."

"And after that, Jim?"

"Let me show you, master," as Jim guided me pass the heaving bodies into the next room.

There slaves were not restrained in any way but were using each other for "practice" as Jim put it, sucking and fucking each other, switching partners whenever a whistle blew. The big difference here was that both male and female slaves were involved in the training.

"This way, a slave learns to fuck on command if that is what a master or mistress may want, and learns how to present himself properly if a master or mistress wants to suck him. Of course, he's still getting plenty of practice in sucking someone off and taking it up the butt, master" Jim said seriously as if he were talking about learning how to play baseball.

The room reeked of sweat, spent cum, saliva, cunt juices, and ass lubricants. Every male slave seemed to have cum leaking profusely out of his ass hole, drool coming out of his mouth, and cum dripping off his prick. Every female slave was wet with cunt juice on her thighs, drool on her chin, and cum deposits in her hair and on her face. All went frenetically from one partner to another, male or female indiscriminately, despite their exhaustion.

"Why so frantic, Jim?" I asked.

"They're trying to earn a meal, master," Jim answered. You have to give five fucks and take five fucks minimum, half with each gender, to get even a minimal amount of slave chow. To get fed to the point where you're not hungry, you need 10 of each, Master, along with at least five suck jobs on a male slave and five oral services of a female slave."

"No wonder you seem to be indefatigable, Jim," I laughed. "Having just a master or mistress, or even both, after this must seem like a breeze."

"Yes, Master, it is. But remember, Master, we sex slaves tend to end up in brothels and we need to be trained for that destination as well, Master," Jim said flatly as if all people ended up being fucked around the clock in a brothel setting.

Jim then guided me to what he labeled "the finishing room."

"Here, master, we get really specialized training," Jim said without explaining further.

I looked around and saw slaves strung up on crosses being whipped, slaves being fitted with biting nipple clamps, slaves being fucked with dildos well beyond the size of any human, slaves rimming obviously unflushed assholes, slaves drinking each other's urine, and, over in one corner, slaves being fucked by horses, dogs, baboons, and even a goat.

"You were here, Jim?" I asked incredulously.

"Yes, Master. Slaves here are trained for any eventuality."

I stared in amazement at what uses a slave's body could be put to and the myriad ways masters or mistresses could creatively use a slave to entertain their most bizarre inclinations.

"Yes, Jim," I commented. "It's better slaves are prepared for whoever might purchase them. It's always easier, I suppose, when you know exactly what to expect," thinking back on the rogue slave trying to wrest free of his rickshaw restraints just because his young owner decided to fuck him in public.

We left the training center shortly after that, but I couldn't help asking Jim, again being led by his tight leash to his genital band, if he had been fucked by an animal or drunk someone's urine while being trained.

"Yes, master," Jim answered with no apparent residuals of shame or guilt which seemed to have little relevance to a slave anyway, especially here. "But I also sucked off a dog and ate a trainer's turd, master. And, oh, I almost forgot, once they had me...."

I cut him off.

"I get the picture, Jim. Completely trained for any eventuality."

"Yes, master," Jim replied as he trotted beside me, his fully erect organ bobbing and weaving as we returned to the main house. There, I ordered him to give himself a series of enemas, freshly lubricate himself, and apply a fresh coat of herbal smelling body oil. I then placed him over the side of the suite's divan and fucked him long and thoroughly, thinking back to all the scenes I had taken in back at the sex training center.

Soon, Jim was full of a fresh load of cum up his ass and, as he cleaned me with his mouth, remembered to thank me profusely for using him. I locked him in the suite's slave cage without allowing him to shower. He could do that later after he had soaked up his master's cum, I thought. It was difficult for me to get rid of the thought of some dumb animal fucking him, but then realized he had been fucked by hundreds and hundreds of slaves in the training center and they were animals too so I dismissed the whole thing from my mind. He didn't seem to mind - why should I, I figured, and it hadn't affected his ability to take a great fuck one iota as far as I could tell.

Later, I mentioned to João what I considered the more gross aspects of Jim's training at his center and the slaves' rather lackadaisical attitude toward it.

"It's good for a sex slave, Christian. Teaches them to appreciate the master they've got."

I thought about João's brief comment and decided he was right. It was probably a necessary and vital part of a sex slave's formal education.

Lunch with João was served by two slaves I hadn't seen before - a short Latino with handsome dark looks and superbly equipped and an Arab man with a handsome well-trimmed pencil-line beard outlining his face who retained all of his black body hair outside of some tasteful trimming around his large genitals so they displayed well.

As I admired the naked waiters, I asked João where they were from.

"The one's a Mexican captive sold to us by a rebel army operating in the southern provinces and the Arab is from a Libyan prison that was selling off their surplus. Nice looking, aren't they?" João explained.

"Yes, and the Arab's unusual - you allowed him to keep his body hair. Very attractive in his case."

"That's what the processors thought when they first evaluated him. His body hair is evenly colored, nicely distributed, and adds to his body features - just like that neatly-trimmed beard adds to his facial handsomeness.

"Are you going to sell them soon?" I asked.

"They're scheduled for the next big auction, but, until then, I keep them around the house rather than in the holding pens."

The two slaves being discussed as if they weren't there reacted by getting bone hard within their tightly fitted genital rings and both started dripping eventually.

"Jesus, João," I said, pointing to the hard-on's the slaves were exhibiting even though they were red in embarrassment at their body's response. "Was it something I said?"

"No, it was what I said," João replied laughing. "A well trained slave seems to always respond to talk about being sold with a big hard-on. My trainers think it's because they think they'll get some sexual relief with an actual master."

"Well, in their case, they're probably right," I laughed. "I doubt a new master or mistress is going to just look at them."

"You're probably right, Christian. Most any owner is going to bed them down first thing, I would imagine, and they'll probably get some relief before he or she's through with them."

With that, we left the two slaves with their dripping hard-on's and João took me to the center where rickshaw and other drayage slaves were trained.

It was outdoors and the first thing you noticed was the immensity of the center. As far as the eye could see, slaves in training were hitched to rickshaw shafts, yokes, and wagon shafts. Many were fitted with right-fitting leather harnesses, mouth bits that pulled their lips back cruelly, reins attached to the sides of their heads, and leather holders that held flexible large plastic dildos deep inside them. Rickshaw slaves had wrist cuffs that could be fastened to the shafts of the carts they drew, while drayage slaves were invariably harnessed in place on the yokes of the wagons they drew. All slaves here were heavily tit ringed, had thick bands forcing their genitals out for full protrusion, and all featured a large ring fitted through their nose septum.

"The nose rings are handy when you want to attach them to a hitching post," João explained, "and the tit rings are useful if you want to bell them. Most owners do - that makes for a nice musical note when they are prancing down the street. The genital band is almost necessary for slaves having to run like them - it keeps their balls out of the way nicely and gets their prick out where people can see it properly."

"What the dildo for?" I asked.

"Oh, to remind them of their status constantly, but also it makes their butt churn when they run - a very nice display. Owners into the finer points of dressage want a prancing step, churning butts, and head upright. The whip handles the prancing step; the dildo takes care of the churning butts; and a tight leash on their slave collars insures their heads are always held upright."

Our attention was temporarily distracted by a slave screaming in agony, still attached to his rickshaw by his wrists.

The trainer was whipping him until blood was running profusely down his back and rump.

"Wasn't lifting his legs high enough," was João's casual comment. "Happens all the time in early training. After a week or so and a scared up back, he'll be prancing around with the best of them. It's hard to lift your legs, apparently, when you have a big dildo rammed up your ass, but it's certainly possible as all our finished products demonstrate."

My eyes shifted to two more rickshaw slaves where their trainer had gotten between the shafts and behind them. They then removed the slaves' dildos, glistening with hot lubricant, and laid them on the rickshaw seat behind them. Each of the slaves had their heads jerked high by a restraining leash connected by their collar to the rickshaw, their prick and balls in full display due to their tight fitting genital bands, and were held in place by the locks holding their wrist bands to the rickshaw's shafts. Both were young and better looking than most drayage slaves - one a pretty brown boy; the other a shiny jet-black man. The coarse looking ugly trainers then proceeded to thrust their large pricks deep into the two slaves right in front of us and fucked away without a care as to who was watching them.

The slaves groaned and shifted as they were fucked, shame and humiliation easily seen since their heads were forced upwards in an unnatural position. Nevertheless, they did nothing but stoically endure the fucking, obviously accustomed to it.

"Is this standard procedure?" I asked, rather astonished at the audacity of the trainers doing this right in front of us.

"Yes, Christian," João answered. "Some of these free trainers think it's their God-given right to fuck any slave under their tutelage anytime they want and view it as a 'fringe benefit' despite the fact the slaves are my property, not theirs. That's why I use slave trainers whenever I can. They only fuck when I tell them they can," João laughed, "and don't dare use my property without permission."

I studied the two slaves being fucked again and noted how accepting they seemed, passing this observation on to João.

"Christian, it's either a big dildo up their hole or a big prick. After a week or so, I doubt if it makes much difference, except most pricks are smaller than the dildos we use. Hell, it may even be a relief to have a prick stuck up you now and then. With a big dildo up you, it's like being fucked every time you take a step anyway - that's why we usually fit all the drayage slaves with them - a constant reminder you're a slave."

Another series of screams were coming from a team of drayage slaves chained together by their necks in a team of eight. One of the eight had fallen in exhaustion pulling the heavy wagon they were hitched to and pulled the others, heavily chained, down with him. All eight slaves were being beaten with a bullwhip until finally they managed to rise as a unit, a mass of blood and bruises by the time they were able to stand upright again. They quickly got back to pulling the heavy load with every muscle in their body outlined in the strain, their bodies spilling rivers of blood mixed with sweat.

"It's tiresome, but it seems to be the only way slaves learn proper breath control, Christian. Drayage slaves' big problem is wind and they've got to stretch their lungs until they can breathe deeply enough to meet the pace demanded. At first, like you just saw, a few flounder around until they get control of their body. After that, they're good for all day no matter how heavy the load or how fast the pace. It's just a matter of getting the body properly conditioned and internalizing a 'can do' attitude about their new assignment."

"And if they don't, Joáo?" I asked.

"Well, it's off to the rendering plant," Joáo replied. "That's what so motivational about our system here. It works so well, we actually lose very few to the rendering plants and, even if we do, these slaves don't cost all that much. But, remember, Christian, we only use the big, strong, stupid, and ugly for these types of slaves. Once fully trained, they're remarkably enduring and generally last for years. They make for a good investment actually - especially at the prices owners can snap them up for these days - even fully trained like the products here."

"Where do most of these slaves come from originally, Joáo?" I asked curiously as I studied their mammoth frames, their layers of muscles, and their massive chests and legs.

"They bred for it, mainly, Christian. Oh, once in a while we spot a freshly enslaved that's naturally built for this, but mainly, they're all bred nowadays. They're brought up to expect nothing else than being hitched to something or other with a whip on their back and a dildo rammed up their butt. That's why we have so little trouble with them despite, admittedly, the exhausting work they're put to each and every day. They've never known anything else, generation after generation. They're happy; we're happy."

"Well, I don't know if happy quite describes falling to the ground exhausted with blood running down your back from the whips, but I suppose not knowing any other life would help considerably, Joáo."

"That and the fact we throw a wench in their cage once a week if they've met their work quota with no trouble. That's where their replacements come from 15 or 20 years down the line."

"You've thought of everything, Joáo," I said in admiration.

"I'm beginning to understand why that slave turned 'rogue,'" I added. "He didn't have the distinct advantage of being bred for his work as I remember."

"That's nine-tenths of that slave's problem, but he can be trained nevertheless," Joáo added.

"I can't believe how much I'm learning here at your ranch, Joáo," I gushed. "I have trouble assimilating it as fast as you're teaching me, professor."

"Is that your way of saying it's time for some rest from all this learning, Christian? How about sampling one of the house boys I don't think you've seen yet. He's a real charmer and extremely well trained and something you haven't experienced yet - a bred slave. He's from a breeding farm in Zanzibar renowned for the quality of their output. He's just turned 19, has had full training as a pleasure slave, and is a beautiful deep brown color. It's high time you tried out a bred slave - a lot of people claim they're markedly superior in bed. I've never noticed the slightest bit of difference between a well trained boy like that Jim you bought and a bred slave, but you be the judge. I'm going to use that Arab man that served us dinner. Shall we entertain ourselves in the garden room, Christian? It's fully equipped for pleasure of that sort."

"Who could turn down a invitation like that, Joáo?" I laughed. "Especially if it's air-conditioned. Damn, it's hot out here," glancing once again at the hundreds of sweating slaves pulling for all they were worth under the unrelenting Brazilian sun and the two rickshaw slaves, covered in sweat, still being rigorously fucked by their trainers. "And those damn whips - don't they ever stop?" I asked as we turned toward the house.

"A good whip is essential to a slave's proper training, Christian. But, I do admit the sound of it gets tiring over time."

CHAPTER 14

The bred slave from Zanzibar was perfect in bed but somehow disappointing. I couldn't fault the slave for doing everything in his power to please me, but despite his expertly trained ass and throat muscles, his willing compliance with anything I wanted, his obvious eagerness to please me, there was something missing. Suddenly, when I was well up his ass for the third time that night, I realized what it was. I really liked the suppressed resentment of a slave like the stud Thor who admitted he hated being fucked but certainly cooperated with it anyway, knowing as a slave there was nothing he could do but please a master no matter what was required. It was the power of forcing a slave to do something he didn't really want to do that turned me on. I remembered Thor groaned in shame and resentment whenever I fucked him although he managed to churn his ass muscles and everything else appropriately. The boy from Zanzibar viewed being fucked like getting his next meal - it was a natural part of his life.

When Joáo asked me the next morning how I liked bedding down a bred slave, I shared my thoughts with him.

"We can test your supposition out when we visit the basic training center today," João smiled. "All the new stock there get fucked right from the start to impress upon them they no longer have any control over their body - that belongs to someone else now. You can rape a brand new one and see how you like it - that way you'll know if your hunch is right or not, Christian."

When we got to the basic training center, the fresh stock had all been given a series of enemas, most had been stripped of all their body hair below their eyebrows, and all were fresh from the showers. Most were in a state of shock, viewing the loss of their body hair and the indignity of being administered forced enemas, along with a heavy metal collar locked around their neck not unlike a farm animal, more than they could bear. Some were openly crying; some were staring into space as if in a trance; some were screaming obscenities; some were testing their sturdy restraints with every muscle in their body. Now the handlers, two to a slave, were fastening them over a sawhorse face down, their wrist manacles fastened to rings set in the floor on one side of the sawhorse and their ankle manacles fastened to rings set widely apart in the floor on the other side. This forced their ass into a fully exposed position atop the sawhorse.

For most of these new purchases, this restrained position caused even more consternation and the maelstrom of protests rose to a crescendo. As a trained slave calmly proceeded down the line of sawhorses and jammed grease up the exposed hole of each new slave, their panic expressed itself in falsetto shrieks and a body covered with cold sweat.

"Pick a slave that's appealing to you, Christian, and then rape the shit out of him. If you like it, your hunch is probably right. If you don't, I'd stick with the bred slaves or something equally well trained. We don't gag the slaves at this stage of their training - we want them to hear their own screams of outrage and despair and realize it doesn't do them one bit of good. They're going to be fucked regardless of anything they do - that's a given for a slave and especially important to learn this early in his training."

João led me over to a bound slave that was still covered with black body hair with the exception of his pubic and ass area which had been shaved to expose these parts to full advantage. Hanging between his legs was a respectable package which looked appropriate for his very large muscular body that featured wide shoulders, a tight bubble ass, a very thin waist considering his chest development, and a nice thick (but collared) neck. He had a heavy three-day growth of beard over rugged jaws, high cheekbones, and deep-set dark eyes. His back muscles, most visible in his position on the sawhorse, were large and well defined like the rest of him. He was covered in sweat - probably from the rage he was expressing with every breath he drew - "you can't treat me like an animal;" "when I get loose, you'll pay for this;" "you sons-of-bitches;" that sort of thing that pretty well matched what all the other new slaves were mouthing off.

"I think you'll enjoy raping this one, Christian. He's just been a slave for a week now, but most of it has been in a holding pen and then shipment down here. He's a construction worker from St. Louis enslaved for failure to pay child support. One of my agents snapped him up - he's just 23, has a good sturdy body, and isn't bad looking if you're into the rugged types. As far as we know, he's hetero - at least he had a wife and three kids before he deserted her, and he's a white boy under all that black hair."

The slave being described responded by a new string of obscenities, directed at both of us, most of them directed toward the fact he wasn't going to be raped by anyone, let alone another man.

João paid absolutely no attention to the slave at all, other than reaching between his legs and roughly squeezed his balls, something the slave had no means of preventing.

"Calm down, slave," João said as he massaged the slave's balls vigorously. "A good fucking is the best thing that can happen to a new slave. Teaches them their body now belongs to a master."

The large white slave bucked and twisted within the tight limitations of his bondage with a fresh barrage of threats and violent objections.

"He's already well lubricated, Christian. Pound his butt until he shuts up but watch that he doesn't bite you. They can't usually restrained like that, but a few real flexible ones have managed occasionally. If it looks like he might, motion for the handler and he'll fasten a tight leash from the ring on his collar to a restraining ring in the floor. But, let me warn you, Christian, this experience is going to be the exact opposite of last night with that slaveboy from Zanzibar."

I slipped out of my clothes and cautiously mounted the hairy slave restrained beneath me. As he felt my prick forcing its way up his chute, he did try to bite me, as João had warned. But he was too well restrained to make that possible no matter how much he bucked and strained. His mouth never stopped as, inch by inch, I forced my way up his ass. In fact, his screams of protest and threats got even louder. After I was fully in his virgin ass, he gasped and tears poured out of his eyes (whether from shock, pain, or rage I never knew or really even cared) and he was so out of breath he couldn't scream as loud as before. When I started a rhythmic pounding, making sure each stroke was full length in and full length out so he would be sure to know I was 'long stroking' him for the full effect of feeling fucked, his screams slowly died out to sobs and within 10 minutes he was reduced to subdued crying as I reached around with one hand and stroked his organ until it was erect - shaming him all the more, especially when I eventually was able to milk him to a full ejaculation which spilled all over his upper thighs and dripped onto the floor beneath him. When I reached my own unhurried orgasm and dumped my full load well up into him, he seemed to know I was filling him with my seed as fresh sobs of despair emanated from a broken man. When I pulled out and cleaned myself with a Kleenex, I knew two things: (1) I had been right - my greatest thrills came out of fucking slaves who resented me doing it but could do nothing to stop it; and (2) raping a new slave was an important and essential tool in breaking him to his new role in life - it demonstrated once and for all his body wasn't his anymore - it now belonged to someone else.

João had watched the whole proceeding as he quietly got an update on the basic training center from his manager there, himself one of João's slaves who had been kept on for his management skills instead of being sold off. When I was putting my pants back on, the manager motioned for a slave trainer to "take over."

As I watched, I saw what that meant as the trainer mounted the back of the slave I had just fucked and began again what I had just finished. The slave groaned in despair as he was once again entered as some of my own cum gushed out of him.

I obviously looked surprised. "Again?" I asked.

"And again and again and again, Christian," João laughed. "We fuck the new slaves until they're bleeding, passed out, screamed out, and don't even have the energy to moan anymore. At least for the next two hours or so with at least six to eight trainers up their butts. After that, when they come to, slavery isn't an abstract concept to them - it's reality and they're beginning to understand that a slave has no more control over his body and his life than a cow bought for its milk production. It's a lesson learned more powerful than the collar around their neck, the rings through their tits, the brand on their butt, or being shorn of their hair. From now on, it's a master's privilege to fuck them, milk them, shave their bodies, squeeze their balls, work them until they drop, hitch them to a wagon, pinch their tits or anything else that might please them. It's all part of a well researched program. The end result is what we call a "broken" slave, i.e., a slave that knows his place in the scheme of things, who does anything he's commanded to do without hesitation, whose privilege it is to bring pleasure to his master, whatever that might entail, and who no longer thinks of himself as anything but what he is - an animal owned by others. This program produces just that, especially when we teach a slave what real pain is, that pain is controlled by their owner, and pain is to be avoided at any cost, no matter what a slave has to do to avoid it. That's why every slave isn't just fucked over and over - they're also beaten over and over until they understand a master or mistress can do this to them for no other reason than they are that person's property. And pain always, without fail, follows asserting a will of your own or even the slightest hesitation in total obedience."

"That explains all the screams and whip sounds and the sizzling sounds of the prods I hear in the next room," I added.

"Exactly," João responded, "although the new slaves are exposed to all sources of pain available to a modern master: electric shock dildos, tit clamps, finger and ball presses, and tooth extraction; along with the traditional forms of slave control: food, water, and sleep deprivation, forced abstinence, additional branding, nose ringing, a ring through your prick; and, of course, the more extreme control measures: castration, burning out a slave's eyes, cutting their leg tendons, or clipping their vocal chords. Of course, those extreme measures drastically hurt a slave's resale value and should be a last resort. Nevertheless, every slave needs to know what can happen if an owner is displeased with their property. That's why we have them sample some of the control measures so they understand their situation and force them to watch actual or filmed demonstrations of the extreme measures. When a slave finds out it's all for real and does happen often enough, there's invariably a drastic change in both behavior and attitude. When that's backed up by them sincerely thanking someone for fucking them or disciplining them, they're usually broken and can live their new life a hell of a lot happier than before. An unbroken slave is invariably a miserable slave. That's why this basic slave training is so important - it leads to a well adjusted, happy slave eager to enter his new life of service to whoever buys him."

By this time, yet another trainer had mounted the slave I had fucked and was humping away, the slave reduced to babbling at this point. Joáo nodded in approval and led me to the next room where, sure enough, discipline, in all the formats useful in training a new slave was in full force.

Slaves screamed horrifically as an electrified dildo was activated well up their ass; as a ball press was tightened; as sizzling hot brands were pressed into their flesh. In another section, chained slaves, long deprived, were desperately begging for a drop of water or a scrap of food. In another section, a few slaves were having nose rings installed in their bleeding freshly-pieced septums while others were having a Prince Albert ring installed in their end of their pricks. TVs throughout the room showed detailed images of slaves being castrated, having their eyes torn out, or having their vocal cords burnt out. In yet another section, new slaves, pumped full of Viagra, constantly stroked to full arousal and dripping profusely, tried desperately to bring themselves off, but it was always prevented. In the largest section of all, slaves were chained to individual posts where trainers competed with each other in how much blood and how wrenching the screams they could get out of the slaves being methodically whipped with all sorts of lashes, scourges, and metal-tipped floggers.

"I'm beginning to understand why a slave is so eager to be sold off," I offered, carefully studying each scene before me. "Most any master or mistress would be an improvement over this I would think."

"That's the whole point, Christian," Joáo laughed. "A teacher friend of mine always claims it's smart to ride around on a broom for the first few days with her students and after that, she lets up a little and they love her."

"These slaves must really love their new masters and mistresses," I chuckled as screams of terror and agony kept up its constant wail.

"You know that fresh slave you raped, Christian? There's a market for 'unbroken slaves' with some buyers. They love the experience of breaking the slave themselves or, in some instances, trying to keep him 'unbroken,' that is always fighting his restraints and swearing at their owner, and that sort of stuff. That turns them on better than anything. We always save a few out for that particular market with the warning they'll have to be kept under heavy restraint and with a prod in your hand the whole time you have them out of their cage. You think you might be interested in a slave like that? I could arrange it easily enough and they're cheap enough - even one decent looking."

"I liked Thor, Joáo. No problems with his obedience or doing exactly what you wanted - on the other hand, he had a way of letting you know he didn't like what you were doing to him but knew there wasn't a damn thing he could do about it other than just bend over and get fucked. That I liked! But keeping them chained and in a cage with them screaming obscenities at you struggling against their shackles - no, I don't think so. Besides, it sounds kind of scary."

"Well, I offered, Christian," Joáo snickered.

With that, we left the basic training center, leaving the same way we had come in. When we left the last room we had been in, the relative silence was refreshing. By the time we got to the first room we had been in, the slave I had fucked was still being fucked but probably didn't realize it - he had passed out and looked like dead meat being pounded on the sawhorse supporting him.

By the time we had worked our way outside again, the birds were singing, the air didn't smell like sweat and cum, and the quiet was relaxing.

"Joáo, it's a great place you have here," I said. "I can see where it's hard to get you to go anywhere else."

"Are you saying you want to extend your stay, Christian?" Joáo smiled.

"No, Joáo, but New York City just doesn't stack up."

CHAPTER 15

Perhaps New York wasn't as interesting as Joáo's ranch, but it was my home and I missed it. Six days at Joáo's ranch had allowed me to see first hand the most interesting aspects of his operation, sample some of his house slaves he wanted me to explore, and bond again with a longtime and wonderful friend.

But the visit was exhausting in a sexual sense. There was so much available meat, each new offering better than the last, that my fears of drying up and dying of exhaustion like a common brothel slave, seemed eminent. Besides, six days was about what I had planned to start with in view of Rico and Beauty penned up at the kennel during my absence. My newly purchased slave Jim had been a nice bonus to the trip, but I did need to get the acquisition to his new home. I wondered how he would fit in with my two existing slaves, but reflected I now had a black, a brown, and a white slave so I could pick and choose according to my mood. How striking the tri-colored threesome would look when I took them out for a walk, all fresh and oiled, being led by their leashes. I imagined them with matching brightly colored neck collars and genital bands

- something like bright red or purple - so everyone would know all three belonged to me.

João's private jet was in use at the time I planned to leave - it was on a long trip to pick up some recent purchases: first Turkestan where one of João's agents had nailed down a great deal on six exceptionally handsome Kurdish house slaves being discarded by a fallen dictator; and then six Polynesian studs being marketed in Samoa. João said that jet had already paid for itself in saved freight charges and was considerably easier on the stock being transferred.

Consequently, I made arrangements for first-class accommodations back to New York City on Brazil's major airline (at a much cheaper fare than any American airline charged) and João made all the arrangements for Jim to go airfreight next-day delivery and to be delivered from the airfreight terminal to my home when he arrived by the delivery service João usually dealt with. Jim's shipment cost was surprisingly reasonable for next-day delivery - about five percent of my first-class ticket, but then, I wasn't going in a huge rack of cramped cages with a plug up my butt and a water bottle clamped to the bars being jerked around by a forklift when I transferred from one plane to another. I would get a couple of decent meals and some wine; Jim would be sucking water out of bottle fitted with a penis-shaped nipple, no food at all, a huge plug up his butt to make sure he didn't dirty his cage, and piss probably raining down on him periodically if he was unlucky enough not to be on the top row of cages.

It was standard shipment for slaves if they were lucky enough to be on an airplane instead of the slave transport trucks used for local transfer. Those types of carriers frequently just crammed all slaves into one huge trailer cage with the open bars allowing for plenty of air (and dust) and open viewing by the public as you slowly bumped from one city to another. It wasn't uncommon for slaves shipped like that to be subjected to a rough fucking right in public by the strongest of the lot; to be bruised and stomped as the slaves were tossed against each other when the truck got up to speed and went around corners or braked hard; and to be covered in each other's shit by the time they arrived since no facilities were ever available. Food was throwing them some slave chow through the bars when the truck refueled and water was being sprayed with a fire hose if the service station had one.

I paid for my airline ticket. Joáo insisted on paying for Jim's freight charges, claiming most slaves he sold were priced to include the airfreight charges if their new owner was from a foreign country.

Slaves didn't need passports or visas, of course, in that they were just property, but were subject, like all goods, to custom fees. Joáo took care of that too as was his practice with an international purchase - in fact that was completely taken of before the slave ever even left his ranch for shipment. I found out the custom charges were modest - only $240 for a valuable slave like Jim. For a common draft slave, Joáo informed me, the custom charges often were as little as 15 or 20 dollars for the U.S.; about $5 for China; $3 for India; and zero for Saudi Arabia, Kuwait, and the U.A.E. who imported slaves by the shiploads these days.

Joáo insisted we spend our last night together, which we did. But Joáo is never happy with just one person for a full night and, accordingly, while we were going at it, two other slaves were kneeling beside the bed in readiness - a green-eyed boy from Kurdistan just graduated from Joáo's sex training center and a pure black boy from Nigeria, recently obtained from a male brothel in London. Both slaves were very muscular, short enough to be easy to handle, strikingly handsome, circumcised, fully trained for bedroom duties, and, as you would expect, quite well hung.

Joáo and I had our farewell fling, but once recovered from that, discovered what the two slaves could offer us. Neither of us were disappointed and, more often than not, all four of us were in Joáo's huge bed at once. Jim, during this time, was receiving a series of enemas in preparation for his big trip, so there was no opportunity to add him to the harem at this point.

Joáo took me to the airport, driving the car himself. His chauffeur followed, accompanied by a handler, in a slave transport truck since Joáo would be accepting delivery of 26 new slaves purchased from a Macedonian prison at a air transport terminal nearby.

"I lucked out on this purchase, Christian," Joáo explained. "Macedonians are snapped up once they're properly trained. Everyone here in Brazil seems to want at least one. They go for their nice builds, their smooth skin, their round typically blue eyes, and their almost innate desire to please. Besides that, most Macedonians are blessed by God when it comes to sexual equipment. Some of them are hard to believe!"

As we neared the airport, I again witnessed the thousands of drayage slaves under the whips, more and more rickshaws being pulled by slaves in full dressage, showy litters being borne high by even showier slave bearers, chain gangs repairing the roads and building new ones; collared construction workers sweating away under the ever present prods and whips; and, the latest fashion, 'display' slaves accompanying their owners from one shop to another, all on short leash, all tightly banded to best display their ample sexual equipment; all exceptionally handsome; and all with bodies that defined masculine beauty. Most were led by a mistress who loved the envious looks she got from her friends and casual observers as the slaveboy carried her packages or knelt at her feet when appropriate. But some were led by a master who enjoyed the raw power and appreciative stares an unusually handsome slaveboy commanded when displayed in a fancy tall, often jeweled, collar with large matching tit rings and a thick genital band. I noted most of these new fads were fitted with gold or silver nose rings to emphasize their animal status.

João saw me studying the 'display slaves' we passed. Most in this district seemed to be owned by women.

"You get something like that started and in no time at all, every women with any money at all has to have one," João laughed. "Those you can market to this new craze sell for four or five times what they're really worth. Then the fad will be over and those mistresses will be off and running to the next fad. But, in the interim - I'm making a killing taking some of my best looking trained sex slaves, fitting them out with a fancy collar and nose ring, putting big rings in their tits, and banding their package so tight it's practically a separate appendage. They're selling as fast as I can get those tall collars welded around their necks and at prices you won't believe."

"What a life!" I commented as we both witnessed an old lady fondling the penis and tits of the 'display' slave of a friend with a decidedly licentious look in her eye.

"Wait until you see what the masters have as display slaves," João chortled. "Handsome freaks if you ask me. But, if you're selling, I keep my comments to myself."

"I saw a couple a few miles back," I laughed. "A white and a black - both were, as you say, freakish, almost. But, handsome bastards, I must say. Both of them showing hard. How in the hell do these slaves stay hard all the time, João? Even at our best, we can't do that."

"Lots and lots of training, my friend," João chuckled. "That, plus never being allowed to shoot off and having a good size plug up your butt to keep your prostate tickled all the time. But still, it's a real skill and highly valued in both display as well as litter slaves."

"And being a house slave at your ranch," I laughed. "It was rare when I saw a normal sized flaccid prick on a slave around your house, João."

Just at that point we passed the largest litter I had ever seen. It looked like it could hold at least four persons if it had to although you couldn't tell because it was completely curtained for privacy. It was made out of a rich hue of Brazilwood trimmed with gold-plated fittings and bright orange silk curtains. It was so heavy it was borne on the massive shoulders of 14 naked bearers - all the same height and muscular build; all jet-black; and all with approximately the same size circumcised genital organs banded by gold which matched their spiked collars. Each of the 14 muscular bearers were fitted with tiny bells attached to their tit rings.

João brought the car to a virtual halt so we could both study the full display.

"That's the owner of the slave market right down the street here," João explained without my asking. "She's really crass and crude and I understand most of the society women here in Campinas hate her guts. She dresses as gaudy as her litter and local gossip has it each of those poor litter bearers with the bells on their tits and those spiked bands around their prick and balls has daily duty in her bedroom as well as heft her all over town on their shoulders. As a friend of mine put it: 'those black boys on her litter have such big butts because the muscles back there have double duty - working their ass carrying the bitch all over town AND working their ass pumping into her old cunt the minute they get her back home.'

Christian, let me tell you, it would take an overseer with a good strong whip to keep those black brutes sweating and panting and humping around the clock. No training I know of would keep a slave doing all that without steady reinforcement."

"But they're all smiles above their collars," I pointed out.

"If they don't show happy, they don't get fed," João chuckled. "That's easy enough to accomplish."

João and I both had a laugh on that one.

"Christian, if you like your boys really black, any one of those trotting along there might be damn interesting in bed," João commented. "All that hard muscle; those big nicely trimmed dicks of theirs swinging around in front of them; and all that sweat running down those shiny black bodies sort of turns you on, especially when you think of any one of those handsome brutes in your bed trying their best to please."

"Jesus, João. I was just thinking the same thing. What does something like that cost down here currently?" I asked.

"A team of 14 with the litter or just one of them?" João asked.

"Just one, João," I answered. "I'm not up to 14."

"It would set you back about $35,000 - no more, and possibly less. Black slaves have gutted the market here currently and the price is going down, not up. It's the breeding farms, Christian. If they keep production up at current levels, they'll be selling for no more than $20,000 in just a few years. The goal is to get the price down to where just anyone can afford a decent looking slave, but the breeders down here love the blacks - they're easy to breed and there's a steady market for the pure blacks at least. Sort of a historical thing down here as much as anything. Now up in New York, they wouldn't have that appeal. Breeders up there are concentrating on whites primarily with some emphasis on mixed bloods, I understand. That makes sense. You breed what's going to sell, Christian."

"It does makes sense, João. Do you think it would be wise to invest some in a white breeding farm close to New York City?"

"It wouldn't have much risk, Christian. And it would have the potential for some solid return on your investment. After all, the only cost are a few handlers that enjoy keeping everyone in line and knowing their place, some good breeding stock to start with, and a little slave chow and water for 15 to 16 years. After that, every year you've got another batch to sell at market. Profits can be enormous, let me tell you, especially if you pick your studs and wenches carefully to start with."

"Well, you ought to know, João," I laughed. "Your own breeding operations must be making a fortune after all this time."

"Christian, I admit I wouldn't have to do anything else to make my fortune, but of course, currently my training facilities and my marketing and import-export operations are also bringing in more money than I care to divulge, but slave breeding is as good an investment as any."

João was the best friend I had ever had, and, I felt sure, I was the best friend he had. Both of us were without family; both of us never had to worry about money; both of us had the same bent; and both of us were not only appreciative of the availability of slaves nowadays, but both of us put them to practical use. (As João put it, we were the ones that kept the economy going!) João had found his niche in the world - Brazil's leading slave firm into slave acquisition, slave training, slave breeding, slave processing, slave marketing, and slave selling. As it turned out, my niche was just about to develop.

João got serious as neared the airport.

"I'll admit I've been studying you, Christian," João started out.

"By fucking me silly last night?" I laughed.

"No, stupid. Sizing you up intellectually and emotionally - not just appreciating that nice fuckable body of yours which I don't want to discredit in any way. Christian, ..." he paused and pursed his lips. "Christian, ... How would you like to work for me, buddy? I don't want to sound ingenuous, like 'work for me' sounds, but, Christian, I really need someone I can trust and understand to run an American office headquartered in New York City. We're currently importing a lot of slaves from all sorts of sources through the States and exporting several times that number to America from all over the world. We've even got American slaves being shipped down here for processing and training and then we ship them right back to sales outlets in the U.S. America's demand for slaves is growing astronomically and demand far exceeds domestic supply and will until the breeding farms are in full operation there. Until then, there's a fortune to be made reallocating the world's slave output to the needs of America's economy. Frankly, it's more than I can oversee properly. I need someone right in the States who will wrest the last penny out of that market and build up the quality image we currently have all over the world. My goal, Christian, is to be not just Brazil's biggest, most profitable, and most prestigious slave operation, but the world's."

"Jesus, Joáo, I don't know.... "

"Shut up and listen, Christian. You're perfect for it. You don't have anything else to do I can see other than fuck those three slaveboys you own. You're clever. I can trust you. You understand now all the uses slaves can be put to. You understand that most any property can be trained to whatever the market demands. You seem to understand that slaves are just property without rights, no different than a horse or a goat. And you don't have any qualms about training them to market needs, buying or selling them, or," Joáo laughed, "just fucking them for a person's enjoyment. You're even eager to invest in breeding operations for the production of local white boys."

"You're laying it on pretty thick, aren't you, Joáo?" I laughed.

"Christian, when I first met you years ago, I said you needed a purpose in life and you agreed. Well, Christian, the slave business is your calling just like it is mine. Once you get yourself involved, you'll forget about these weird philosophical notions you entertain about 'finding yourself' and all that crap. Hell, you have 'found yourself' and it's with a whip in your hand buying and selling human livestock. You believe in destiny, Christian?"

"Yes," I admitted. "Things do seem to happen according to some plan or another."

"God's will or just destiny. Hell, I don't know. But your destiny is as clear to me as it should be to you. Just say yes to working for me and destiny is at your doorstep, Christian," Joáo stated quite empathically.

I was overwhelmed and didn't know what to say.

"Here's the deal, Christian. My agents in the U.S. will ship me fresh stock after clearing it with you. You can add any new agents or sources you want and get rid of any agents that aren't pulling their own weight. You'll get 5% on each slave shipped down here from the states or, with bred or previously trained slaves, a 5% transfer rate when you resell them in American markets. With all stock shipped up to you, including Americans trained down here, you'll get 5% of their selling price in the U.S. I'll rely on you for quotas of nationalities, colors, sizes, and shapes, based on what's selling for top prices in the U.S. I want you to buy up breeding farms already in operation and set up some new ones using American studs and breeding wenches, using my capitol to set the whole operation up. In return, I'll get 5% commission on output from those farms when they're of prime selling age. The more you sell (or breed), the more the make. The more I sell to you, the more I make. It's a win-win situation and a deal that doesn't lead to arguments later on. The best part is - we'll both make so much money we'll be billionaires many times over within a decade and my firm will be known as the best on God's green earth. And you, Christian, will be proud as anything, making more money and having greater respect than your own father ever dreamed of."

It was Joáo's last comment that made up my mind. I had always felt guilty living off inherited wealth, even when I knew I could never spend it all, no matter what I did or didn't do. I wanted an identity of my own and Joáo was offering it to me on a golden spoon.

"Is there a retirement plan? And what about medical insurance?" I joked.

"God Almighty, Christian," Joáo practically exploded. "Is that a 'yes'?"

"Yes, Joáo, and fuck the retirement plan. I was thinking the other day I'll probably have the life span of a brothel slave if I don't stop fucking slaves three or four times a day."

"You're growing up, Christian," Joáo said. "But I have that same worry about fucking myself to death," he laughed.

We embraced and I now worked for Joáo de Silva - an arrangement that lasted for many a year and, as Joáo had predicted, made us both multi-billionaires within 5 years, not the 10 he had predicted.

CHAPTER 16

SIX WEEKS LATER:

Parading Jim, Rico and Beauty on a stroll through Central Park was satisfying, although not quite the sensation I thought it would be. The trouble was, everyone else seemed to have the same idea and with stock just as good looking and sexually exciting as my three slaves. True, having them outfitted alike (bright orange collars and genital bands fitted tightly with matching gold plated tit-rings) and each a different fully shaved hide color (black, brown and white) along with the different leash placements (one slave by his collar; another by his tit ring; and the third by his genital band) created some stares of appreciation and admiration. But many other masters and mistresses had put thought and energy into both what they were displaying and how they were displayed. Some people too poor to own even one slave came to the park just to see what was being shown that day - the same people that routinely go to the slave markets to see what new stock had come in overnight. The advantage of Central Park viewing was you were viewing the best the markets had to offer; the advantage of visiting the slave markets was that you could actually feel the goods for yourself, including stroking a big buck into a full dripping erection and no one seemed to care much even knowing you couldn't afford to buy the goods being offered that day.

Six weeks ago, when I had arrived back in New York, I freshened up in my townhouse and then walked down to the kennel where I had boarded my two slaves Rico and Beauty. They squealed in delight when they first spotted me through the bars of their cages, both springing full erections just from seeing their master again. They seemed to be in good shape, obviously having been fed, watered, and exercised properly in my absence. Their dripping erections indicated the kennel had followed my directions in keeping them shackled within their cages so they couldn't get themselves off no matter how needy they got over the entire week I had been gone. I must say the place was reasonably clean (they and their cages had obviously been hosed down recently) and the other kennel occupants seemed well taken care of despite their cramped cage confinement.

As I paid the kennel's fees for maintenance of the two slaves, I asked the owner how his business was doing.

"Thanks for asking, sir," he answered politely. "I can't complain and we're adding some services almost every month that's beginning to add to the bottom line."

"Well, there's more and more slaves every day here in New York and a certain percentage of those are going to have to be kenneled now and then for their owner's convenience," I commented, "but what are the new services? I thought a kennel just fed, watered, and exercised slaves primarily. Oh, maybe a nice grooming occasionally."

"More than occasionally, sir," the kennel owner laughed. "Some owners are bringing in their stock just for that during the day without ever renting a cage. But we now offer some services you used to have to take your stock to a slave market to get: tit ringing, re-collaring, genital banding, ear ringing, personalized decorative tattooing and branding, installation of a penile ring or a ring through the slave's nose septum, circumcision, and, our latest new service, deballing."

"Well, that is handy," I complimented the owner, "but just how many are turning their studs into eunuchs these days? Oh, I know they used to back in Roman times and in the Old American South, but you're giving up their studding potential and probably some strength and energy in the long haul - at least from what I've read."

"Well, one good stud can service 500 breeding wenches if he's managed right," the kennel owner laughed, "so not every slave stud needs to reproduce anyway. And, if a slave is nutted after he's fully mature, there's a lot of debate about just how much strength and stamina you really lose when you castrate them. A lot of aggression, probably, but not much actual strength, it seems. A slave that has trouble controlling their aggression and gets a little feisty sometimes or seems to need too much whip to make him easily managed is a natural candidate for the procedure in my mind. It's easy enough to do and they recover quickly if it's done properly. Not much risk and a lot to gain in certain cases. We're able to offer the procedure for only $300 plus boarding charges for three days. That's peanuts compared to what slaves cost. Not too much more than we charge for a nice clean nose ringing these days."

"But, how many owners are actually forking over the money?"

"For a nose ringing or a deballing?"

"Ball removal," I answered.

"We're doing about 3 or 4 a day anymore. We've got a whole new wing added just for that procedure and then caging them for recovery. Not many, compared to the numbers brought to us for banding their slave's packages or ringing their tits, but still worth our investment in the new facilities. The biggest growth has been in installing a large ring right through a slave's nose septum. Owners like it as a great control device - it's easy to hook a leash to, for example, or to fasten a slave to a retainer ring - but a lot of them just like the look it gives - it's catching on fast, sir. You might want to consider it for these two," he said, looking down at my own slaves kneeling beside me, my two leashes fastened securely to each of their genital bands.

Once the bill was paid, I led the two slaves to their "home" a short distance away, each walking behind me in perfect coordination the length their leash allowed. As they had been trained, each kept their heads upright with lowered eyes, their posture erect, and remained totally quiet. But both slaves were obviously very happy to be uncaged at last, sniffing the fresh air, practically prancing in their step, and proudly flaunting their bodily assets as others walking glanced appreciatively at them, especially their huge erections, still hard and dripping.

Along the way, I was amused by a stocky middle aged black master, more fat than stocky actually, fucking his muscular light-skinned Mexican slave. The handsome slave, looking to be in his early twenties, was bent over a park bench while his master fucked him, his collar leash tied to the bench itself so make sure he stayed bent over properly. The young slave's owner was quite well hung and it seemed amazing the slaveboy could handle the pounding without being split in two, but other than the slave groaning and grimacing in pain, he seemed to be handling it, no doubt well broken in to his master's huge tool by this time.

I stopped, along with some others out for a stroll, to take in the little show and noticed by own two slaves glued to the scene being played out in front of them, their pricks quivering and dripping copiously. It didn't take much to get them all excited, I thought, after spending a week in a cage shackled so they couldn't bring themselves off. It would make them appreciate me all the more when I put them to regularly servicing me again now that I was back in the city.

When we got back to my townhouse, their nostrils quivered the minute they entered the door, conspicuously smelling my new property, Jim. Slaves are uncanny that way - any new slave in 'their' territory seems to send out a unique scent that is instantly noticed. Both Beauty and Rico's pricks quivered in response. I took them downstairs and showed them Jim kneeling in his cage and explained I had purchased the slave while in Brazil. He was an Oklahoma boy, a few years older than them, and specially trained as a sex slave in a renowned Brazilian slave training center - owned and operated by my friend Master João who had fucked both of them here in this very house on his last visit.

"It will be nice to have a pretty white slave to service me when I want in addition to you two colored ones," I smiled. "A master always enjoys a nice variety at hand."

That's all I said in that there is no need to explain anything to a slave, let alone justify anything. I didn't give a damn whether they felt threatened by the new arrival or not - it was their job to accommodate me - not the other way around.

Whether there was tension or not at the new competition for my usage I don't know. I never saw any of it and by that night all three were serving supper, each dripping hard, each eager to do anything requested without hesitation, and each properly subservient. When I ordered Jim to fuck Rico for my entertainment, he mounted Rico eagerly while Rico, on his hands and knees, took Jim's large organ up his chute without a moment's hesitation and, as Jim pumped away, got a big smile on his face even before I ordered Beauty to get beneath Rico's body and suck him off. Later, I had Jim suck Beauty off and, after those initial introductions to each other's bodies, the slaves got along fine with each other. My timing was perfect. The two kenneled slaves hadn't been allowed to cum in over a week; Jim hadn't been allowed to cum for the entire time he was in transit. No wonder they liked what each could do for each other - albeit under my complete direction, of course.

Within a week, I had the three slaves fitted out in matching collars and genital bands and was using them as display slaves as well as bed bucks.

But, I didn't spend all my time fucking the three slaves at my disposal. Now that I worked for João, I had to prove he was right in trusting me with his business interests in the United States.

The first order of business was to invest in some long-term breeding operations. Either buy out some existing ones that showed promise or set some up of my own. This required checking out what was ongoing and could be purchased if one had the capital. I had capital practically unlimited - João had in essence given me a blank check!

The first purchase was a small operation located on a farm not thirty miles north of the city. They owned two magnificent Nordic blond studs who were being mated regularly with a small stock of only 300 light colored American breeding wenches. It was a new operation, but promising with a first crop of 280 now two years old and the second crop of 283 (some twinning had occurred) now only a year old. Already all 300 breeding wenches were successfully impregnated and seemed to be well into yet another healthy pregnancy. The farm was fast running out of capital and could barely feed the stock on hand. If they didn't find a well-financed buyer, it was doomed. They sold to me at a great price which included all 563 products so far, all 300 wenches (all under 21 even now) with their swollen bellies, and the two studs, only 20 now with at least a few more years of constant fucking left in them. Assuming we could count on 250 surviving stock a year by the time they were 18 or so, we would have an inventory of 4000+ potential slaves for the marketplace without any expansion at all. All would be white or near white and, looking at the breeding stock, all would have a good chance of being big, handsome, sturdy, well hung, and, by the time they would be marketed, totally compliant and biddable to anything a buyer might want. I kept the managers in place instructing them not to spare any cost in feeding the stock or keeping them healthy in a clean, well-supervised environment with good medical care and lots of exercise each and every day. I assured them their original concept was sound - they just lacked the money to pull it off. Now they could, but, of course, the profits would be mine, not theirs. But they would have a good well-paying job, they would be doing something they liked (overseeing breeding), and they could take pride in a good saleable product if they continued doing their job correctly.

As the new owner, I did request the two Nordic studs be sent to my overnight hotel room from the farm's rutting sheds. They arrived that evening freshly scrubbed, completely douched, and well lubricated. Both gave no resistance as I ordered them onto their backs with their legs spread wide and up over my shoulders for a good fucking, but they had that same look of controlled rage and abject shame I had so enjoyed in Thor, João's white stud down in Brazil. Again, I decided it was the resentment I enjoyed as much as the tightness of their well-greased ass chutes.

Next, I bought up six similar small operations, also nearby where I could keep an eye on them. One was a breeding operation up in Harlem run out of some old tenement buildings, now gutted with barred windows and doors allowing vast open spaces for corralling the breeding stock, holding pens for the products, and exercise and training facilities aplenty. This 'Harlem breeding factory' as it was called specialized in American blacks and had an average yearly output of about 300 a year. It had been in operation for six years now, but was also running out of capital. Another was in nearby rural Pennsylvania and turned out whites primarily. A third was in New Jersey and utilized Porto Rican slaves as the breeding stock. A fourth, in the worst areas of the Bronx, was a little bigger but produced only draft slaves, using some of the cheapest slaves currently available as breeding stock - Haitian slaves. A fifth, also in New Jersey, was even bigger - about 500 a year output - but utilized imported slaves as breeding stock - Russians, various Balkans, and Greeks. The sixth was trying something different - only pure blacks from equatorial Africa were in the breeding pens. The goal was to eventually market shiny pure blacks with huge muscular builds without a trace of genetic mongrelization. Altogether, these six operations should produce a good 2000-3000 quality slaves a year for the markets a decade and a half down the line.

João was very pleased with these initial acquisitions on American home soil but urged me to get into some really large operations, similar to those in Brazil, Mexico, and Poland, all of which he had at least part ownership in. Those three countries were currently the world's leaders in huge single-site slave breeding operations. João wanted ours to be even larger.

Consequently, I went to the South and Midwest where land was a lot cheaper and non-slave labor costs could be minimized. I settled on Southern Missouri for one mega-factory and Mississippi for a second. Both locations had good rail and interstate connections for shipping the products to market swiftly and at relatively low cost, had land enough to grow the crops to feed the products, and where it didn't get so cold you would have a lot of heating costs over the winters.

The one in Missouri was constructed from scratch to handle over 10,000 wenches in full production, could handle over 150,000 products without crowding or security problems, and would offer full training facilities for every age slave during their development to market. It cost over $125 million to build the simple, but secure facility and another $500,000,000 just for the breeding wenches alone, but, down the road, the profits would be staggering for the long-term investor. The Missouri operation was to handle primarily whites and half-breeds of various types. Consequently the majority of studs were white boys but a few were blacks, browns, and even a particularly handsome well hung Asian boy and a striking Polynesian. I designed the operation to be the breeding farm of the future with its emphasis on lost cost per output, huge production outputs each month, and the finest training facilities around. The goal was to market big, healthy, handsome slaves completely trained for their new life who would bring top dollar on the auction block.

The one in Mississippi was even bigger and we utilized a facility bought from the state - a huge prison they had no use for now that slavery was replacing prison sentencing. With some simple remodeling, the old prison made an ideal slave breeding facility: the old license-plate stamping machines were replaced with rutting benches; the hospital was turned into a birthing center; the exercise yard remained intact as did the thousands and thousands of cells. What used to be isolation and execution were now devoted to training; the prison farms now were slave powered and produced all the food needed plus some for sale; and, of course, clothing issue was no longer needed at all. The remodeling was designed for a minimum of 15,000 broods producing at least one slave a year on the average, meaning, over 15 years, it needed to hold 240,000 products in various stages of being ultimately prepared for market. It was designed to be the largest breeding operation in the U.S. and, along with the Missouri operation, able to fill up to 40% of American's slave markets when it was in full production 17 to 18 years from now. Besides being bigger, the Mississippi operation specialized in the production of black slaves primarily, although the actual color of the product varied from jet black to a majority of nicely hued browns to some light colored, almost yellow, quadroons. These latter products were practically indistinguishable from those from the Missouri operation to the untrained eye.

All of this required huge sums of "up-front" money (billions and billions) but João never flinched. Just the opposite - he lauded me constantly for doing exactly what he had in mind and reminded me continually I was not only paving the way to becoming one of America's richest men over time but that my father couldn't even fathom how successful his son was to become.

As it turned out, João was exactly right in his forecast. The problem was - we were too successful. Eventually we churned out so many appealing products the market was gutted and prices started to fall dramatically. But, just as João and I started to panic, slave prices dropped to the point where the American middle class could fit a slave purchase or two into their budget. When that happened, the market for slaves exploded and prices leveled off and then began a slow upward trend.

As Joáo said, "If you're big enough, you can outlast any market." But neither of us foresaw the clouds gathering!

CHAPTER 17

SEVEN YEARS LATER:

No one could have foretold what happened to those most responsible for America's prosperity. Someone in the highest places clearly thought the nation's wealth was drifting away from their control and decided to act boldly.

The nation's national security laws, passed hurriedly and with little consideration years and years ago in a near panic, had proven most useful when it came to doing what the government wanted done without the inconvenience of running it though Congress or putting it up for a vote. When a 10% federal tax on slave sales proposed by the Administration to finance the huge cost of their wars in the Middle East (still going on from way back in 2001) failed to get through Congress, the privately owned slave businesses were declared a terrorist threat and America's top security risk and all of them were nationalized overnight. Now all unsold slaves were property of the national government who "could secure the nation's safety by determining to whom they would be sold and what use they would be put to once sold." By this time, almost 40%

of the nation's population were slaves if slaves had been counted in the census (which they weren't of course, being property), so it was a massive transfer of wealth from the private to the public sector in an instance since 10% of those slaves were currently owned by these slave businesses. To quell any public outrage at this enormous property theft, the move was accompanied by an executive order to immediately reduce the price of slaves by 15%, a move that was acclaimed by the vast majority of people, even though this was almost immediately changed to a 10% reduction and, six months later, the price was actually raised by 10% from the original prices. The only parallel was when Saudi Arabia nationalized their vast oil fields from foreign ownership back in the 1950s.

Thus, without warning or premonition, all of our capital had gone to the national treasury. Joáo's and my own huge fortune in domestic slaves had literally disappeared.

To the slaves, it made little difference who got the money from their sale. Of most importance to them was what sort of a master or mistress they would end up with and what they would be required to do under new ownership. But to the slaves' (previous) owners, it made a hell of a difference. One, all our hard earned money was gone. Two, our potential earnings base was wiped out. Three, (which made the first two mean nothing really) we were charged as terrorists to justify the deed and promptly enslaved ourselves, probably to insure we were out of the way and couldn't protest or take it to the courts.

I was seized, stripped and collared the very next day in my townhouse in New York immediately after the charges of terrorism were read to me by the federal agents. The minute the agents caught sight of my naked slaves Jim, Rico, and Beauty, they roughly leashed them by their genitals bands.

"Your sex slaves?" I was asked.

I nodded affirmatively.

With that, one of the agents took out a marker and placed a big "SS" on the front and back of the three slaves.

"Put them in a separate van and make sure they're put in the holding pens for next Thursday's sale. That's when we're selling off a big batch of already trained sex slaves we've accumulated."

The last I ever saw of my three different colored bed bucks was as they were abruptly dragged by their balls to a van outside somewhere, looking totally bewildered by this sudden turn of events.

João was seized under the extradition laws the U.S. administration had worked out with Brazil in obvious preparation for their bold move toward nationalization of the slave industry. (This extradition was easily arranged since Brazil got to keep all of João's huge holdings inside their borders, including thousands and thousands of slaves - a real windfall for the Brazilian government!)

All of the captains of the domestic slave industry were sequestered in the vast slave pens used by the Federal government outside Washington, D.C. for those charged with anti-terrorism activities. Those just working as non-slave labor in the formerly private slave operations (the training supervisors, the breed masters, the security forces, the disciplinarians, the marketing specialists, the purchasers, etc.) were enslaved along with us, but were generally sent to the nearest local slave pens, often the very facility where they had previously been employed.

Thus, within a week, João and I found ourselves together again - this time sharing a small pen in a stifling hot warehouse stark naked with collars around our necks, our bodies totally shaved, our tits ringed, a thick band tightly fitted around our manhood, a fresh brand on our left butt check and right pectoral, a big plug up our asses, and slave identification marks on both our inside wrists, our upper right arm, and our left ankle. We were sharing a pen since former co-owners were caged together so the government knew where we were coming from.

"Well, at least we have an idea of what to expect," João whispered, since slaves weren't allowed to converse in a normal tone, even when caged. João wiggled his hips around in an effort to better accommodate the huge butt plug forced up far inside him.

"That's putting a positive spin on things," I said. "My tits are so sore from these rings it almost makes me forget about the pain from the brands. Still, I guess we're lucky we're alive, João. I saw the two blacks that ran our breeding operation down in Mississippi beat to death when they fought and kicked over being ringed and banded. Seems like the government doesn't give a damn how valuable the property is that they seized. They're acting like they can afford to just dispose of slaves that are giving them a little hassle initially."

"They're just amateurs at handling slaves, Christian," João said. "That much is clear. We would never tolerate the loss of two good looking blacks just because they resisted a little at their initial processing. These guys just view us as government surplus, not something that's worth quite a bit when marketed properly."

More and more cages were filled as the government continued its nationalization of the industry. João and I were hosed down every other day, body shaved once a week, and milked once a week for some reason or another. Our processing was routine - getting acclimated to being fucked regularly by the guards, standing in various positions hours on end while trainers fondled, stroked, pinched, and poked every part of our bodies without us flinching, and learning how to best display our bodies for inspection by a potential buyer once we were up on the auction block. To both of us, we knew the routine by heart and these yo-yo's weren't into anything new or novel as far as the marketing of slaves went.

Like slaves all over the world, our biggest concern was our future ownership. Who would buy us and for what purpose? That was the main concern of any thinking slave. Both of us weren't spring chickens anymore. João was nearly 35 by now and I had just turned 32. Nor did we have the nicely defined musculature of most slaves their forced exercise regimens produced. We were both well hung, we were both handsome, and we both had a lot of sexual experience for whatever that was worth. Probably due to our advanced age, the government didn't want to spend any money in specialized training for us. Hence, we weren't sent out for special sex training, or draft slave training, or schooled in how to bear a new owner's litter or pull a rickshaw. Just obedience training, posing on command, and basic hygiene and body grooming were our only classes at the government's holding center. We both knew the government didn't think they were going to get much for us at our age.

João and I were scheduled for the same auction. Two days before the big event, we were given a series of enemas and chained out in front of our cage for customer inspections. Twelve hours a day for two solid days we were fondled, stroked, jerked off, fucked with dildos, had our nipples pinched and squeezed, our teeth examined, had our balls hefted in endless palms, and even had our eye lids peeled back as they checked us out. Occasionally, we were unchained, and, led by a leash connected to the band around our balls, taken to a nearby tent which contained a bed, a fucking bench, and a place to kneel. There, in relative privacy, a potential buyer could fuck us, have us fuck him or her, have us suck them off, or do anything else they wanted to explore. I got fucked by an old fart in his 60s, a gangly teenager with pimples, and sucked off a dried-up 70 year old (which took forever). I had to fuck two females - one an old hag in her late 50s and another about my age. Joáo seemed to be more interesting to customers: he ended up having to fuck five females ranging in age from their early 20s to one at least 75; got fucked by six men (all of whom were rather gross), and had to suck off a whole series of young boys along with their fathers who apparently wanted their sons to have the full experience of a big public slave inspection.

By the end of the two days of stock inspection, Joáo and I both had sore butts, sore pricks, and sore tits. We had swallowed enough cum to dull our appetite for slave chow (which had taken us a while to get used to). When the big day of the auction came, we were almost relieved in that hordes of people wouldn't be pawing our tits, squeezing our balls, and stroking our pricks endlessly.

Joáo and I were early in the auction line-up due to our age. The best (prime stock) was saved for last. Joáo was up on the block, stroked by the handler to a full erection prior to being presented. He was bid on by an middle-aged Arab sheik, a black man in his mid-twenties, an Asian man who looked to be at least 70, and a rather fat woman in her mid-fifties. The fat lady bought him for only $35,000 - a knock-down price usually reserved for slaves fairly well worn out.

I was next up. Bids were slow as I was turned around and made to bend over to best display my hole, then turned around again and ordered to thrust myself out to best emphasize my erect banded organ. Eventually, bids were made by that same middle-aged Arab sheik that had bid on Joáo, the same black man in his mid-twenties, a crude looking white man in his forties, a black woman in her late 30s, and another Arab man I couldn't see very well due to the strong lighting. This time, the black man made the winning bid and I was his for only $33,000 - a very low price due to my age and the fact Joáo was hung better and more muscular than I was.

As it turned out, João's mistress lived within three blocks of my new black master - both in a middle-class neighborhood where slaves were kept either in a basement cell, a cage in the attic, or a pen in the garage if there was room. This didn't surprise us - slaves at the price we sold for usually ended up as "only" slaves of middle class people who couldn't afford the better quality slaves but who at least had something to warm their beds and do their dirty work. Because of our owner's proximity, João and I saw each other occasionally, usually when our owners had us out shopping with them (presumably to carry their packages) - totally naked and being led by a leash attached to one or another of our body fittings. We even had a chance to stealthily converse on those occasions when our owner was busy doing something else and we could whisper a few words to each other. João was kept busy all the time cleaning the house, doing all the yard work, doing all the laundry, and fucking his mistress three and even four times every day. She seemed insatiable, he claimed, and he was kept drained dry. Despite that, the old bag offered his services to others occasionally, especially people the old lady owned money to.

"But, at least I'm still doing the fucking," João said with a big smile. "Instead of fucking myself to death drilling my pretty slave boys' asses down in Brazil, I end up fucking myself to death humping that old bag," he laughed. "If I don't die first of overwork doing all the laundry, cleaning and yard work the old bitch manages to come up each and every day."

"My fucking days are over, João, I'm afraid," I declared. "My black master is just 23, I found out, and horny as they come. I'm his only outlet as far as I know and he fucks me, either up the ass or down my throat, no less than five times a day. I don't know where he gets the stamina to fuck like that, but he does. Besides that, João, he's hung like a horse so my ass and throat are sore all the time. I can barely swallow the handful of slave chow he gives me twice a day and my ass is always so sore it's hard to sit down when I get a chance. I haven't fucked anything since he bought me and the only time he let's me get off is when he milks me every Saturday night for his 'special treat' as he calls drinking a cup of my hot cum. He's threatening to sell my services to some of his black friends, but, João, I'm not sure he has any friends. His biggest thrill seems to be taking me out on walks leashed by my balls so all his neighbors can see he now owns a white slave. Joáo, did you ever realize what all those slave's lives were actually like that we sold by lots of thousands?"

"Yes, Christian. Remember, I trained them for that life from the womb on and broke the rest of them to their new lives in my training centers. I knew what a slave's life was like and, frankly, so did you. Both of us didn't have to concern ourselves about it - we were on the other side of things."

"Joáo, did training them prepare you for your life now?" I asked, suspicious I already knew his answer.

"Yes, Christian. I knew exactly what to expect and it's worked out about like I thought. I adjusted fast enough and I'm sure you did too. I just didn't know whether I'd end up fucking a mistress or being fucked by a master. Doesn't matter too much, I guess. When I'm sold off, it's most likely going to be to a master anyway. That is, if I'm lucky and can still be fucked to justify my cost. The day will come, Christian, when we're both sold off as common draft slaves and then it's learning to live under the whip. You know that as well as I do. It's the plight of any slave losing their youthful charm."

"Joáo," I answered thoughtfully, "it's strange, but I don't mind it as much as I thought I would. I guess I knew what to expect and it's not as bad as I thought. In fact, I kind of like getting fucked regularly and I do feel valued. Perhaps this is my purpose in life - the purpose you always claimed I needed. At any rate, you're right about being sold off eventually. But I'll face that when it happens."

"What choice do you have, Christian?" Joáo laughed. "In the interim, enjoy what you can. That's what I'm doing - even if it is fucking that old bag - beat's no fucking at all - and boy, does she like it!"

About that time, our owners returned and, with jerks on our leashes we were led away in opposite directions. That was the last time I ever actually talked to Joáo. He was sold off to a new master who routinely had all his slaves muted by having their vocal chords cauterized. But Joáo now was being fucked just like me - he just couldn't talk about it anymore.

Strangely enough, we both met again. Our owners had tired of us at about the same time in that we were now in our 40s and showing it. It was getting hard to maintain a good erection anymore and our bodies just didn't have that youthful appeal anymore. Consequently, we were both in the same lot of 100 being bid on for draft slaves by an agribusiness in California.

We spent the last ten years of our life under the heavy whips of overseers out in the boiling sun 14 hours each and every day harvesting everything from sunflowers to corn to wheat to cabbages. We worked in heavy chains side by side and, despite João's inability to talk anymore, we figured out a way to communicate effectively. All in our chain gang were placed in the same cage at night so we were able to snuggle up and use each other sexually when we had the strength. In some ways, we were right back where we started - in each other arms sharing all we had in common.

We even died together as it turned out. A thrashing machine top-sided in a ravine and our gang, chained together by the neck while clearing out that ravine, were squashed by the huge machine, it's hot engine burning our flesh beyond recognition.

Our death was ironic in that the thrashing machine was one of the last in use in the United States. Slave labor was so cheap by now, the fuel to run the machine cost more than the slaves. After that, slaves did all the thrashing - as well as everything else!

ABOUT THE AUTHOR

Bill Smith is a prolific writer of various fantasy tales about slaves and the huge variety of fictional societies and settings that foster them.

Bill Smith is also the author of **Bates Training Center**. Available at Amazon.com, TheNazcaPlainsCorp.com or your local bookstore.

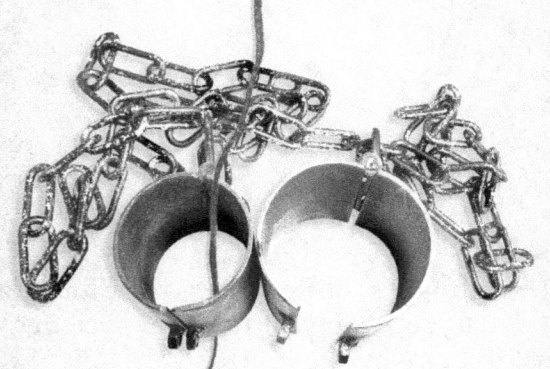

BATES
TRAINING CENTER

A NOVEL BY
BILL SMITH

A
BONER
BOOK

SMITH

BATES TRAINING CENTER